GUN BRAND

GUN BRAND

Wayne C. Lee

SAGEBRUSH
Large Print Westerns

First published in Great Britain by Jenkins
First published in the United States by Arcadia House

Published in Large Print 2009 by ISIS Publishing Ltd.,
7 Centremead, Osney Mead, Oxford OX2 0ES
by arrangement with
Golden West Literary Agency

British Library Cataloguing in Publication Data
Lee, Wayne C.
    Gun brand.
    1. Western stories.
    2. Large type books.
    I. Title
    813.5'4–dc22

ISBN 978–0–7531–8268–0 (hb)

Printed and bound in Great Britain by
T. J. International Ltd., Padstow, Cornwall

CHAPTER
ONE

It was the kind of night a man might choose to ride if his mission were dark and secret and meant only for the eyes of the night wind and the whispering buffalo grass. It was the kind of night Dan Blake chose to come to Winner.

The moon had deserted the sky and clouds had moved stealthily to cover the southern and western stars. Blake sat his saddle easily, but there was an attentiveness about him that belied any slackening of caution. He rode, head cocked forward, trusting his ears where his eyes were practically useless. Then he reined up, for the soft breeze was bringing smells that meant people — smoke and the sweet clean fragrance of newly turned earth.

He sat for a long time looking into a blackness that told him nothing his senses of hearing and smell could not detect. The grass moved about his horse's feet, a soft whisper that only a man of the prairies could appreciate. A dog howled mournfully somewhere ahead, the sound skimming the prairie to strike at Blake like a tangible thing.

After a time he turned his horse to the right and began a slow circle of the town he could not see, had not seen, yet knew as well as if he had lived there. They called it Winner, and it would be like dozens of other little towns he had passed through the last day or two on these Nebraska plains. One main street, perhaps two or three side streets, half a dozen business houses, a dozen or so homes. A town rising out of the prairie, part of it built from the prairie sod itself.

Blake swung to the north along the east side of town, checking the time. Past two o'clock. He nudged his horse closer to the town until the first buildings became dimly visible.

Cautiously he moved on until he was on the north side of town, then the northwest corner. There he stopped again, listening carefully for a sound from the sleeping town. Off to the south along Prairie Creek or in the sand hills just beyond, a coyote voiced his loneliness and a dog in town answered.

Blake kneed his horse into a dim trail that was meant to be a street. Still no sound came from the town, no warning from the dogs that there was a night rider in the street. He stopped once more as buildings rose on either side of him. There would be a picket fence, a two-story frame house, the biggest and finest home in Winner. His eyes swept the skyline and picked out the house off to his right, towering above its neighbors.

Quietly he rode toward it, made a half-circle, and came to the back. There he dismounted and ground-reined his horse. There was no picket fence behind the house, but there were three strands of barbed wire. He crawled through the fence and crossed the freshly plowed yard. Apparently Ben Evans had planted a garden in the spring, and the barbed wire was to keep out wandering cattle.

Blake pounded on the back door. He wondered if he could rouse Evans. The first knock brought no response, and he hammered the door with his fist again. A dog beside the soddy across the fence from the big house began to bark excitedly.

The door opened a few inches and a voice came from the deep darkness inside. "Take it easy, stranger. Make a false move and you're a dead man."

"Put up the artillery," Blake said. "I'm looking for Ben Evans."

There was a moment of silence; then the door opened an inch wider. "Who's looking for Ben Evans?"

"Dan Blake."

Another moment of silence; then the door swung back. "Come in," the man said. "Anybody see you?"

"Just the dog across the fence. If I hadn't had to pound so hard I wouldn't have stirred him up."

"I got here as soon as I heard you. It's nearly three o'clock. I wasn't sitting up for you, not knowing when you'd get here."

Blake could see very little in the pitch-black hallway. He was able to make out no more than a dim outline that looked something like a sorghum barrel set on stub posts. Evans, he remembered, was built like that.

"It was your idea having me sneak in this way," he said irritably. "How about a light?"

"Back here."

Evans led the way through another door into a dark room. He shut the door and, striking a match, touched it to the wick of a kerosene lamp on a desk. It was then that Blake got his first look at Ben Evans in ten years.

Evans was clad in a nightshirt inadequately covered by a short robe. He still reminded Blake of a sorghum barrel. Short, fat, bald-headed, piercing black eyes — those were the things Blake noticed and, oddly enough, they were the things he remembered. The years had not changed Ben Evans.

Blake glanced around. The room seemed to be an office. There were two chairs, a desk, a safe in the corner, but the outside wall did not hold a single window. Blake brought his eyes to Evans.

"Mighty careful nobody sees a light in here, aren't you?"

"Nobody must know about your coming here," Evans said.

"Then why did you send for me?"

"I have my reasons." Evans shoved a chair toward Blake. "You've still got ideas about getting the Lazy B back, haven't you?"

"I've had ideas like that ever since I left the country."

"All right," Evans said. "You pick an apple when it's ripe. This apple's ripe."

"I don't savvy." Blake sat down, studying the fat man. "Last I heard Ed Harms was still running the Lazy B."

"He still is." Evans lifted a cigar from a box on the desk, rolled it between his fingers and laid it back. "Trouble is, he's not running it the way some people around here want to see it run."

"Meaning you or Adam York?"

4

Evans shrugged. "York isn't the only power in the country now."

"He was the kingpin when I left."

"He's still big, but when you left, there wasn't anybody to fight him. It's different now, with settlers coming in like they have been the last three or four years."

"Are the homesteaders stomping on his tail?"

"Well," Evans said evasively, "he's been able to handle them so far. But time's running out on him."

Blake leaned forward in his chair. "I was just a kid when it happened, but I don't forget easy. York hired Harms to kill Dad, then moved in and took the Lazy B. There wasn't any law here then. Wasn't even a town within a hundred miles. I was too young to do anything about it, but I never forgot how it was. I aim to square it."

"I figured you were a chip off the old block," Evans said, satisfaction slurring his words. "That's why I sent for you."

"I still don't savvy," Blake said. "I thought from the way your letter read that things had changed."

"They have in a way," Evans said. "The nesters are crowding York. He's had to fight for the river and even his sand hills. You'll remember there are some rich valleys down in those hills. York moved the surveyor's rocks so nobody can find the corners of the sections. They're afraid to file because they'll probably wind up with a quarter-section of hills and blow-outs. But the real trouble's been along Prairie Creek. Some have tried to settle there, but York made it so hot for them they sold out. Now he owns their land."

"Well then," Blake said disgustedly, "he's stronger than he ever was."

"Now you're going off half-cocked. Adam York is in real trouble. There are a lot of settlers hanging on, just waiting for a chance to whittle him down to size. York's had plenty of bad luck and he's had to borrow. He's getting in pretty deep." Evans moved around the desk and sat down. "Your dad and I were good friends, Dan. You'll never know how bad I felt when I heard about his death. I was in Omaha at the time. When I got back here, you were gone. Wasn't anything to Winner then but three covered wagons, a tent and a soddy. Well, ever since then I've been waiting for the chance to help get the Lazy B back into Blake hands. I say the day has come to take it."

Blake studied the fat man. Ben Evans wasn't telling everything. But what was he holding back? "You sure talk a lot without saying anything," Blake said finally.

Evans folded his pudgy hands across his belly. "I've said a lot and I'll say more. York has his hands full with the Flying Y. He isn't big enough to hold everything. If he lets anything go, it will have to be the Lazy B."

"York won't let anything go, unless he's changed an awful lot."

"He hasn't changed, but he's in a bind. The Lazy B rightfully belongs to you. But I say you don't deserve it if you won't fight for it. And if it comes to a fight, you'll get plenty of backing."

6

Blake rose and walked across the floor, then turned and pinned his eyes on Evans. "Just what kind of backing can I expect from you?"

"A banker can give a lot of backing if you play it right, Dan. I'll see to it you have what money you need to fight York when you take over the Lazy B."

Blake eyed the banker for a minute. It had been ten years since Harms had shot his father, and ten years was long enough to change a country. He had discovered that today. But he doubted if a million years would be enough to change a greedy bullhead like Adam York.

"I'll need guns, not money, to do this job," Blake said. "Maybe you'll hire some guns for me."

Evans smiled thinly. "I can't do that. I can't let people know I'm taking sides. You've got all the guns you'll need right there on your hip."

"Against York's crew? Evans, you're weak in the head."

"I know what I'm talking about," Evans said. "York's at the breaking point. One good gun is all it will take."

Blake dropped back in his chair, scowling. He had no liking for this. He had supposed when he'd received the banker's letter that Adam York was finished. But it wasn't that way at all.

"Evans," he said, "you'll have to do better than this."

"It's you who will have to do better," Evans said. "Quit worrying about York. Your first job is to get Harms out of the way."

"Maybe if I go out there and yell 'Boo,' Harms will tuck his tail and run."

"I think he will if you yell loud enough. He's been having trouble with his crew, I hear."

"If I brace Harms, it'll mean a fight," Blake said flatly. "What kind of law have you got here?"

"Tough," Evans admitted. "They call the sheriff 'Slinger' Ainsley. He didn't get his nickname tossing pebbles. But you can stay out of trouble with the law. Harms will bluff."

Blake studied the bland face of the banker carefully. This just didn't add up. "Evans, are you afraid of York?"

The banker sat upright, startled. "Why should I be afraid?"

"It looks mighty funny, you having me sneak in here at night like this."

"I'm just being careful," Evans said. "I wanted to talk to you before anyone else did. As a banker, I have to appear to cater to both sides. Anyway, I don't want anyone to know you are here until you face Harms. Now that I'm looking at you, I think you could have ridden in right in broad daylight. Nobody would recognize you. You don't look anything like you did as a boy."

"The only reason I came back is to settle with Ed Harms and Adam York and get the Lazy B back into my hands," Blake said. "I didn't have to sneak in to do that."

"I think maybe you did," Evans said. "You mustn't tangle with York until the sign's right." His eyes raked Blake's long body, now slack in the chair, and rested a moment on the low-holstered gun on Blake's hip. Then he lifted his gaze to the bronzed, lean face. "You'll do,

8

Dan. Once York has been stripped of Harms and the Lazy B, his empire will crumble. So you've got to start on Harms."

Blake rose and walked to the door. "That's exactly where I intend to start."

"You're going out to the Lazy B now?"

"Any reason why I shouldn't?"

Evans rubbed his hands together. "No. Just be careful."

"I've come too far to be careful now," Blake said.

He opened the door and left the room.

CHAPTER
TWO

Quiet still gripped the town when Blake crossed Evans' plowed yard and crawled through the barbed wire fence. The eastern sky was lighter now, forecasting the glaring ball of flame which would rise into that sky within the next hour.

The dog across Evans' fence woke and barked sharply again as Blake swung aboard his blaze-faced sorrel, but he reined away without further challenge.

Blake rode out of town, circling around to the south of it. The light was stronger now, the pinkish hue in the east becoming red. He found a fence blocking his way, and beyond the fence he could see the black earth of a plowed field. Not far distant was the squat outline of a sod house. A light was burning in the window. Like most farmers, this homesteader was an early riser. In an hour or two he would be in this field, working his team hard before the sun got too hot.

Swinging around the fence, Blake found a trail leading south. This land, as he remembered it, used to be the northern border of the Flying Y and Lazy B range. Sometimes the cattle had wandered farther north, for there had been nothing in those days to stop them except the riders who tried to keep them from straying too far.

Now homesteads lined the trail on both sides. A few were fenced, but most were not. As the light grew stronger, he noticed abandoned soddies, their windows gaping holes in the walls. He knew he was close to Prairie Creek, and these empty sod houses bore mute testimony to the effectiveness of Adam York's iron-handed control of the country. Slinger Ainsley might be a tough sheriff, but he had not given the settlers protection against York's riders.

Before reaching the creek, Blake swung southeast across unfenced land again. Off there eight miles or so lay the Lazy B, a place that had been home to him through most of his childhood years.

Blake came to Prairie Creek just as the sun shot its first dazzling days over the horizon.

He crossed it, and the Lazy B buildings came into sight. They were changed but little from the way he remembered them. The barn and corrals beside the stream were badly in need of repair. But the house, a frame building standing on a knoll south of the creek, was a sturdy structure that showed no sign of deterioration.

Blake nudged his sorrel into a trot and pulled up beside a horse standing at the hitchrack. He swung down and, with his horse between him and the house, lifted his gun enough to make sure it was not stuck in the leather. Then he stepped around the hitchrack.

At that minute the screen door of the house banged open and a big man, more than six feet tall and well

11

over two hundred pounds, strode through the door. His brown hair was streaked with gray, and there was a tuft of almost pure white at each temple. The wrinkles of his forehead were set in a permanent frown, and his short nose seemed to pull his upper lip away from ragged teeth in a permanent leer.

"Howdy, stranger," the man said in a coarse voice. "Been riding far?"

"Far enough," Blake said.

Ed Harms was heavier than Blake remembered, and there had been no hint of gray in his hair ten years ago. But the thing that interested Blake most was the fact that Harms didn't know him. Harms had worked on the Lazy B for two months before his fight with Jim Blake. He had been better acquainted with Dan Blake than any man now living on Prairie Creek. Yet Harms didn't recognize him.

"Looking for somebody?" Harms asked.

Blake nodded. "Yeah. And I've found him."

Harms came down off the veranda. "What's on your mind?"

"Take a close look at me."

Harms scowled as he moved toward Blake. "Your face is a little familiar. But I ain't . . ." His jaw dropped. "You're young Blake, growed up."

"That's right."

Harms' eyes touched the holstered gun on Blake's hip, then lifted to his face. A sneer pulled up one corner of his mouth. "One Blake tried to throw a gun on me, and I showed him. I reckon I can show another one."

Blake's fingers bent into hooks.

12

"You'll show me," Blake said, "or you'll pack your war bag and get."

Harms grinned, confidence surging through him. "Then I reckon I'll have some fun. You didn't ride up here thinking I'd tuck my tail and run, did you? This range belongs to Adam York, in case you didn't know."

"I know." Blake's eyes didn't waver. "You killed my Dad, and that fixed it so York could steal the Lazy B. You've run it for ten years for York. That's long enough."

The grin faded from Harms' lips. He motioned toward Blake's horse. "Light a shuck out of here, Blake. I drilled the old he-wolf, all right, but I had my reasons. I don't have any reason for plugging the pup unless you make one."

"You've had your chance to pull out with a whole hide," Blake said. "Now I'm through talking. You can draw or drag."

The fingers of Harms' right hand curved above the butt of his gun. For a moment he stood that way, motionless, his eyes raking Blake. And Blake, thinking back, remembered that Harms had been a cocksure man who swore he never made mistakes. In this moment it was obvious he hadn't changed.

Blake caught the muscle twitch in the man's face as he started his draw, and then Blake's gun hand swooped down with all the speed and muscular co-ordination that he possessed. He was a killing machine, made so by long hours of practice that had prepared him for this moment.

Gun thunder rocked the quiet morning air, one shot a split-second before the other. Then Blake held his fire as he watched surprise wipe the triumph from Harms' face. The bullet from Harms' gun had spurted dust into the air a foot in front of Blake.

Blake waited, his finger still tight on the trigger. Then he saw that the job was done. Harms tried to hold himself upright, to pull strength out of his dying body for a second shot, but the strength was not there. His gun fell from slack fingers, and he toppled forward into the dust and lay still. It was the way Jim Blake had fallen ten years before.

Blake turned back to his horse, sliding his gun into leather. He was remembering Evans' words, "They call the sheriff Slinger Ainsley. He didn't get his nickname tossing pebbles."

As he moved to his horse, Blake heard the pounding of hoofs and wheeled to see three riders racing toward the house from the east. This, Blake guessed, would be the Lazy B crew. Possibly they had been returning to headquarters, or they might have been working close enough to hear the shots.

Blake swung into the saddle, knowing that he had to run or tangle with three men he had no reason to fight.

He tickled the sorrel's flanks with his spurs. The horse stretched into a run along the river bank, heading west. A yell went up as the riders behind discovered him, but the sorrel was fast, and although he had been traveling a good part of the night, he wasn't tired. Blake glanced back to see one rider wheel off toward the house, while the other two kept on coming.

14

For half a mile Blake kept to the level ground bordering the little stream, but he saw that he wasn't pulling away from the men behind him. So, with a slight tug on the rein, he angled the sorrel toward the sand hills. His pursuers, a quarter of a mile behind, saw his intention and whipped up their mounts in an effort to catch him before he reached the hills. They shortened the distance but were still three hundred yards behind when Blake reached the first hill.

The sand hills that lay close to Prairie Creek were small and didn't offer the chance to elude his pursuers that the bigger hills farther south would. So Blake rode straight on, making no effort to throw off pursuit.

A half-mile from the creek he turned to look back, and satisfaction swept over him as he saw the riders sitting their horses on top of the first knoll. They had given up without getting a good look at him.

Blake eased the sorrel up but kept him at a steady lope into the bigger hills.

CHAPTER
THREE

Blake wasn't sure how far he rode, but it was past noon when he topped a hill and saw a sod house in the valley below. Apparently a nester had settled here, but the soddy was deserted now. There was no barn or corrals, nor was there the slightest sign of life around the house.

Blake rode boldly up to the front door. Like so many soddies, there were no windows, only holes in the walls into which little wooden doors were fitted whenever a storm threatened. Most of the home-steaders were too poor to buy windows. Even the front door of this soddy was sagging from just one of its leather hinges.

There was no way for Blake to tell how far he was from the creek. He had swung back to the west after leaving Harms' men and must have paralleled the stream. He looked at the hills bumping the horizon in every direction, but there was no movement. This would be as good a place to rest as he could find. He had not slept since yesterday afternoon when he had pulled the saddle off his sorrel and taken a nap before making his night visit to Winner.

Dismounting, he ground-hitched his horse while he looked around. The soddy had but one big room, and there was nothing left in that room but a crude chair with one broken leg. Ten wards from the door of the soddy was a dug well. He remembered that water in these low valleys was usually within ten feet of the surface.

He was thirsty, and he crossed to the well. Sod had been piled up in a circular wall around the well, and the wooden framework of the windlass with the handle still intact was in place over the well, but there was neither rope nor bucket.

Fighting down his thirst, he turned to his sorrel. It was his own fault that he had to go thirsty. He had been so intent on getting to the Lazy B to settle with Harms this morning that he had neglected to check his canteen. Now it was almost empty. He started to unsaddle, then checked himself. There was nothing but sagebrush and bunch grass in sight. Where would he hide his sorrel? A horse standing in front of a deserted soddy would invite investigation from any passer-by, lawman or not.

With one jerk, Blake tore the door off the one leather hinge that held it, then, stripping off the saddle, led his horse through the opening. He brought in the saddle and stacked it and the bridle in a corner. The sorrel didn't like the confines of the walls, and he especially disliked the low ceiling that prevented him from tossing his head. But after a few disgruntled snorts, he became passively silent.

Blake propped himself in a corner where he could see through both the door which was in the south and the east window. There, hunkered down against the wall, he dropped into a troubled sleep.

It was late afternoon when he roused. He rose, stretched, and went outside for a look around. Everything was peaceful and quiet, but the gnawing of thirst was becoming intolerable. He thought of saddling up and riding on until he found food and water. But he decided against it. This was a good place to hole up. If a posse was on the prowl, they would be watching for him to move tonight. He still had a little water. He would make it last. And tomorrow night after the town had cooled off, he would slip in to see Evans.

He went back inside the soddy and flipped out his bedroll. He had some dry biscuits in his saddle bags, and he ate them, but they only added to his thirst. He took a sip from his nearly empty canteen, then stretched out and tried to sleep.

It was light when he awoke. He rolled up his blanket, thinking there would be no breakfast for either him or his horse. Sometime today, perhaps near noon, he'd move on.

It was mid-morning when he saw them first, a half-dozen horsemen riding along the crest of the hill to the east. He didn't question their identity. Six men riding that close together meant a posse. And they'd be looking for him. He was glad he had brought the sorrel inside the house. They probably wouldn't give the soddy a second look when they didn't see a horse around.

But he soon realized he had guessed wrong about Sheriff Slinger Ainsley. The posse was lost to sight the minute it dropped off the hill, and when it came into view again, the riders were moving straight up the valley toward the soddy. Blake had one of two choices: to surrender or to run. And intuition warned him not to surrender to Slinger Ainsley.

He carried his saddle outside, hoping the posse wouldn't catch the movement. The riders had come up a knoll half a mile to the east and were moving at an easy jog, apparently not expecting to flush their prey there.

Quickly Blake bridled the sorrel and led him outside. He shot a glance up the valley in time to see a hand lift into the air and motion toward him, and the next minute the posse rolled forward at a full gallop. Blake swung the saddle up, jerked the cinch tight and stepped aboard. The posse was still a quarter of a mile away but coming hard.

The sorrel wanted to run, and Blake gave him his head for half a mile until he reached the west end of the valley. He climbed a hill and dropped down out of sight of the sheriff's men. Swinging around the shoulder of a hill, he headed north. Leaving the hills would be the last thing the posse would expect him to do.

He rode hard, knowing he must be getting close to the creek. Topping a knoll, he looked back. There were no horsemen in sight. He grinned, thinking how easily he had lost them, but there was actually little hope in the thought. They wouldn't stay lost long.

He kicked the sorrel down the slope and came across a trail running out of the hills from the south. Blake guessed that it was a trail used by Flying Y punchers in their trips into the hills southeast of the ranch headquarters. It was not a heavily traveled trail, but there were fresh tracks in it now.

The traveling was easier after he took to the trail. Speed was what he wanted, enough speed to give him time to see Ben Evans before the posse discovered its mistake and caught up with him. Evans had sent for him. Now maybe the banker could find a way out for him, although logic forced him to admit it was a slim hope. He could not escape the conviction that Evans was playing a sinister game of has own. Still, slim hope or not, it was the best bet he had.

There was, of course, one other possibility. He could keep riding and probably get out of the country without any more trouble. But running went against his grain. Now that he was there, he'd see this job through. And this job wouldn't be through as long as Adam York was alive and owned the Lazy B.

Suddenly he jerked up on his reins, right hand dropping to his gun. A riderless horse was blocking the trail as Blake rode down a sandy knoll. Kicking his sorrel forward, gun half drawn, he located the rider fifty yards down the trail.

His first thought was that the man was dead, but when he came up, he knew better. The man was lying beside the trail, apparently where he had fallen from the saddle. His new range duds tagged him as an Easterner, a dude.

Blake swung down and dropped to one knee beside the injured man. He was young, about Blake's age. With a quick hand, Blake searched for the wound and found it, low in the left shoulder, almost in the chest.

Whoever had thrown that slug had been playing for keeps. The wound was barely bleeding externally but, judging from the look on the man's face, Blake decided something was seriously wrong inside. The man, he judged, had only a few minutes to live.

He rose to get his canteen and then remembered it was empty. He started to turn toward the stranger's horse when the man opened his eyes and mumbled something. He lifted a hand, his eyes pleading. Blake dropped back on his knee.

"Something you want to say, stranger?"

The man's lips worked, finally forming the word, "Ambush."

Blake nodded. "I figured that. Who did it? Why?"

The man's head moved slowly back and forth. "I'm new here." His eyes closed and he was silent, his head rolling to one side.

Blake waited a minute, then felt of his pulse. The stranger would tell him nothing more. He stood up, reached for his horse's rein, then stopped. The man was a stranger in this country, and he was almost exactly Blake's size. Neither of the men on the Lazy B nor the sheriff's posse had seen any more of Blake than his horse and clothes.

Quickly Blake stripped off his shirt and pants and boots and exchanged them for the dead man's clothes. He worked as fast as his fingers could fly. Still it seemed to take an exasperatingly long time to dress the dead man. Ainsley and his men wouldn't be all day getting back on Blake's trail.

With the change complete, including everything but his gun, Blake turned to the stranger's horse. There was a cold lump in his middle as he mounted the new horse and looked back at his sorrel. That sorrel had been almost as much a part of him as his right arm. But he was a marked horse. Maybe later Dan could reclaim him. Now he had to be left for the sheriff.

He lifted the bay he had mounted into a run. The new clothes were almost a perfect fit but they weren't comfortable. They were loud and garish, definitely not what he would have bought if he had been outfitting himself new.

The draw he was following suddenly opened out into the flat bottom land bordering Prairie Creek. To his left he noticed a ranch layout. There was a big white frame house surrounded by cottonwoods and two barns with a labyrinth of corrals. That would be Adam York's Flying Y.

Suddenly it struck Blake that he had no idea whom he was impersonating. To all purposes, Dan Blake was back there in the sand hills dead. Pulling his horse down, he searched through the pockets of the new coat and pants. There was a letter in his inside coat pocket. He took it out and glanced at it. It was addressed to Clyde Carson. That, Blake decided, must be the man he was supposed to be. He stuffed it back and went through the other pockets.

In a back pocket of the pants he found a wallet. Opening it as he jogged along, he found an identification card indicating that the bearer was Clyde Carson from Delmont, Ohio. He whistled softly. A tenderfoot, all right. He wondered what Carson had been doing in the sand hills. And who would want to kill a greenhorn?

Blake lifted the envelope from his pocket again and pulled the letter from it. It was short and written in a scrawl that was almost illegible, but there was no mistaking the signature at the bottom. *Adam York!* Blake's eyes went back to the top.

> "Dear Clyde,
> Your offer is greatly appreciated. You bring the money and I'll see that you get a chance to try your hand at this business.
> Yours truly,
> Adam York."

Blake shoved the letter back into his pocket. This put a new light on things.

CHAPTER
FOUR

The sun had swung well to the west when Blake came in sight of Winner.

He rode down the center of the main street and reined up in front of the restaurant, feeling the curious stares of the bystanders. Dismounting, he carefully and laboriously tied a knot in the reins around the hitchrack, remembering that he had a role to play. Passing himself off as a tenderfoot was going to be the biggest job he had ever tackled. A slip at the wrong time could throw him into the arms of Sheriff Slinger Ainsley.

Blake felt the eyes of the people in the restaurant from the second he stepped through the door.

He took a table against the wall, sitting so that he could watch the door, and gave his order. While he waited, he looked over the few people who were in the restaurant. He knew none of them; he hadn't expected to. When he had left ten years ago there had been only two ranches along Prairie Creek, and it wasn't likely that many of the men who had worked on those ranches would still be in the country. Ed Harms had been, but then Harms had been York's right-hand man. Not many men stayed with York long.

The only person who held Blake's attention was a girl seated at the counter. Her blue eyes possessed a sharpness that seemed to go through Blake when she looked at him. Her hair was brown but it held a strong reddish tint. She was talking to a tall man who sat beside her. He was twice her age, probably her father, Blake thought, and he wondered about them, for they seemed to fit here no better than he did. They obviously were neither farmers nor ranchers.

His meal came, and he dug in with relish. But in spite of his ravenous appetite, he was aware of the glances that the girl and her companion at the counter were sending his way. There was more behind those glances than just the idle curiosity that prompted most people to look at him.

Then, his meal half finished, he saw the girl slide off her stool at the counter and move gracefully across the room. He kept on eating and didn't look up at her until she touched the back of the chair across the table from him.

"Mind if I sit down?" she asked.

He gave her a long look. She was pretty, all right, but it was her eyes that caught and held his attention. There was a fire there such as he had never seen in a girl's eyes before.

"Go ahead," he said. "Don't mind if I finish my dinner, do you?"

She slid into the chair. "Of course not. You seem to be real hungry. Been a long while since you've eaten?"

Caution kept him from giving a quick answer.

"Had a light breakfast and missed dinner," he said.

"Where are you from?"

He shot a look at her. Her smile was friendly enough. But she should know better than to ask a stranger where he was from before she introduced herself. Then he realized that he couldn't challenge her on that count. An Easterner wouldn't know it was bad etiquette to ask a stranger where he came from.

"Ohio," he said. "What about you?"

Her brows pulled into a little frown. "You think I don't belong here?"

Blake shrugged. "I didn't mean that. But nobody has been in a town like this for long. They had to come from somewhere."

She laughed easily. "I hadn't thought of it that way. We're from Iowa. My father has an office in the back of the bank building. I'm Hazel Thornton." She held out her hand like a man.

Blake laid down his fork and gripped her hand. "Clyde Carson," he said, finding the words strange to his tongue.

For a moment he thought he caught just a flicker of surprise in the girl's eyes, but then it was gone and he wasn't sure he had seen it at all.

"Going to stay in Winner long?" Hazel Thornton asked, her smile inviting.

"Might," Blake said. "Haven't decided yet."

"If you do decide to stay, look us up. Maybe we can throw something good your way. Dad is in the real estate business."

She got up then and went back to the counter.

26

He finished his meal. As he ate the last mouthful, he had the odd sensation that someone's eyes were pinned on him. He glanced quickly at Hazel Thornton and her father at the counter, but they had apparently lost all interest in him. Turning slowly, he studied the other people in the restaurant.

He saw who it was then, a girl standing in the doorway. She was slender, an attractive figure in her cream-colored Stetson and leather jacket and riding skirt, and she was quite tall. Her eyes were blue, but they were soft and entirely lacking in the piercing quality that he had seen in Hazel Thornton's. She was staring at him unabashedly as if she knew him, but was waiting for him to make the first move.

Blake dropped his gaze and picked up his coffee cup and drained it. He didn't know her and he didn't want her to think he did. The less he said, the better. He rose and stepped over to the counter to pay. Then, turning to the door, he came face to face with the girl. She was still looking at him in that straightforward way. He nodded, touching the brim of his hat, and moved past her into the sunlight.

Blake was starting toward his horse when he saw half a dozen riders move into town from the south. His steps faltered as he realized this was the posse that had been trailing him. He moved forward again, knowing that the slightest hesitation now might throw suspicion upon him, but he'd have nothing to fear if he acted out the part he had assumed. He was Clyde Carson from Delmont, Ohio.

The posse came down the street at a walk, the last man leading a sorrel horse with a body tied across the saddle. Blake paused at the hitchrail, fascinated with the thought that for the time, at least, it was Dan Blake who was being brought in dead. Sheriff Ainsley stopped his men in front of a small building just north of the restaurant. Blake saw the sign, "Sheriff's Office," painted above the door.

A crowd collected around the posse like iron filings gathering to a magnet. People came out of the restaurant and hurried toward the sheriff's office. Blake saw Hazel Thornton and her father in the crowd. Then, from the brick building at the corner of the block, Ben Evans came, moving swiftly and easily for a man so fat.

Evans stopped at the edge of the crowd as though reluctant to ask the question that had apparently forced him to hurry over there. But no such hesitation held back the man with Hazel Thornton.

"I see you got him, Sheriff," Thornton said. "They told me they had made no mistake when they gave you the star."

Ainsley cuffed back his battered Stetson, looking at Thornton a little sourly. He was a tall man, long-muscled and long-boned, and there was something about his brittle stare and the way his thin lips made a long, down-curving line that told Blake he was all Ben Evans had said he was.

He shook his head now, saying in a strong bass voice, "I didn't get him, Thornton. We found him dead."

"Found him?" Thornton's face showed surprise. "You mean your posse didn't kill him?"

"You can't kill a dead man," Ainsley said.

Ben Evans had pushed forward now and was standing close to the sorrel, looking at the body.

"Who is this, Ainsley?" he asked.

"It's the man we want," Ainsley said. "We flushed him out of Trowley's old soddy over on York's range. We could have sneaked up on him if we'd had any idea he was in there, but he had his horse inside the house with him."

"You're pretty good at figuring things out after it's too late," Evans said.

Blake felt a chill run over him. Evans had seen that it wasn't Dan Blake on that horse. He hadn't seemed particularly distressed when he had thought it was Blake. But now that he knew it wasn't, he was visibly shaken. Had Evans wanted Blake killed? Blake switched his eyes to the sheriff, wondering if Ainsley knew whom he was supposed to have brought in.

"I supposed you'd have guessed he was in that soddy, Evans," Ainsley said angrily.

"Maybe," Evans said. "But what I want to know is who killed this man."

"I don't know," Ainsley said. "We chased him when he left the soddy. Then we lost him. When we found him again close to the creek, he was plumb dead."

"Here comes Doc Gentry," Evans said. "Maybe he can tell you something."

"This hairpin has no use for a doc now," Ainsley said.

"Doc's also the coroner," Evans said.

Ainsley leaned back against his horse to wait for the man shuffling through the crowd.

Blake took a good look at Doc Gentry. Doctor was the last tag Blake would have hung on the stooped man moving up to the sheriff now. His hair was iron gray, almost white, and obviously hadn't been cut in months. It hung down over his shirt collar which, judging from the looks of the rest of his clothes, must have been hopelessly dirty. He was clean-shaven except for a drooping mustache. His skin was shriveled and his eyes were sunk far back into his head. Blake had the feeling he was looking at a walking dead man.

Gentry ran surprisingly quick hands over the body, examining the wound Blake had looked at earlier.

"What about it, Doc?" Ainsley said.

"He's been dead no more than two or three hours," Gentry said.

The sheriff snorted. "Tell us something we don't already know, Doc. We were chasing him this morning. He was plenty alive then."

"Bring him into my office," Gentry said. "I'll examine him there."

"Nothing to examine him for except to measure him for his coffin," Ainsley said. "A couple of you fellows carry Blake into Doc's office."

Blake, standing on the fringe of the crowd, masked his face against the shock of surprise. How did Ainsley know that Ed Harms' killer was named Blake?

Thornton had moved up close to the sorrel to watch the men take the body off the saddle. "Are you sure this is Blake?" he asked.

30

Indignation was plain on Ainsley's face. "My eyes aren't so bad that I can't tell a horse and an outfit of clothes when I see them. I told you we got a good look at him when he high-tailed it from the soddy."

"There are a lot of clothes like this," Thornton said.

"And I suppose you think there are a lot of horses just like that sorrel." Ainsley motioned to a stocky man with dark skin and black hair and eyes who had ridden with the posse. "Klitz, you chased Blake off the Lazy B yesterday and you saw him again today. Any question in your mind about this carcass being Blake?"

"No," the stocky man said. "Same size, same clothes, same horse. Maybe you know how to sell a poor sucker a blow-out and make him think it's the Garden of Eden, Thornton, but I know horses. That's the same sorrel."

Blake, still standing on the edge of the crowd, realized that his position was not as good as he had thought. For some reason, Thornton seemed convinced that the body was not that of Dan Blake. Had he known Clyde Carson? If he had, Blake's hours in Winner were numbered.

Evans watched the men carry the dead man toward a little building not far from the sheriff's office; then he turned to face Ainsley. "I want to know who killed that man if you didn't."

"He's dead, and it saves the county hanging money," the sheriff said irritably. "I don't care who plugged him. Good riddance, I say."

The sheriff started to turn away when his eye caught and held on Blake. The sharp eyes of Slinger Ainsley weren't going to miss that worn gun belt and smooth-handled gun. The sheriff pushed his way through the crowd to Blake.

"Just ride in stranger?" he asked.

Blake nodded. "About an hour ago."

"Ever see that dead man before?"

"I didn't see any dead man on the trail in from the east," Blake said, hoping the sheriff wouldn't pin him down.

Blake knew he was in deep trouble. If Ainsley kept asking questions, he'd find out enough to make sense to him. Blake looked around quickly, his mind groping for an escape.

His eyes met the blue eyes of the girl he had seen in the restaurant doorway. There was still that inviting look in them, and this time he didn't ignore it. He grinned at the girl, and she smiled back and began pushing toward him.

"The dead man wasn't found on the trail east of here," Ainsley said. "He was in the edge of the sand hills south of the creek. If you came in on the east trail, you couldn't have seen him."

"How else would you expect me to get here from McCook?"

The girl reached Blake then. "Were you looking for me?" she asked.

"I guess I was," Blake said

"Just who are you, stranger?" Ainsley demanded.

"Tell him, Clyde," the girl said.

"The name's Clyde Carson," Blake said, "if it's any of your business. Clyde Carson from Delmont, Ohio."

Ainsley wasn't convinced. "You're a little off your range, aren't you?"

"I'll vouch for Mr. Carson," the girl said. "Pa sent for him."

Ainsley sighed. "That's good enough for me. You'd better get him out to the Flying Y, Kerry. No telling what might happen to a tenderfoot like him here in town."

Blake turned away so neither Ainsley nor the girl could see his face. This was a little hard to take, and sharp eyes like those of Sheriff Ainsley might see more than Blake wanted them to see. He knew now who had come to his rescue. But Kerry York was the last person in the world he would have called on for help had he known.

CHAPTER
FIVE

Blake followed Kerry York down a well worn trail and splashed across a stream. They crossed the first bottom, knee deep with grass, and came up the little rise to the second bottom where the Flying Y main house stood. As they pulled up in front of the hitchrail, a puncher came out of the dusk of the porch and reached for Kerry's reins. He was about thirty, Blake judged, with sharp features and sandy hair that needed the attention of a barber. His eyes, a peculiar faded blue, were pinned on him instead of the girl.

Kerry dismounted. "Clyde, this is our foreman, Sid Saylor. Sid, my cousin, Clyde Carson."

Blake nodded and turned his attention back to Kerry. For the first time he knew what relation Carson had been to the Yorks.

"Take care of the horses, Sid. Supper will be late. Pa will want to talk to Clyde, anyhow." She turned to Blake, who had stepped out of the saddle and had come to stand beside her. "Sid usually eats supper at the house. That way Pa gets a chance to talk things over with him. The other meals Sid eats with the crew in the cook shack."

Going up the walk and across the porch with the girl, Blake reconsidered his position. He had been in danger in town when Kerry York had given him a hand. Now he wasn't much better off. Even if York didn't recognize him as an impostor, a cousin of Kerry's would be expected to know about relatives back in Ohio. Blake would have to pull leather on that one. And if Adam York ever discovered he had taken in a Blake, no means of correcting that mistake would be too quick or brutal to satisfy him. He had hated Jim Blake, and he'd hate Jim Blake's son just because he was his son.

There was one alternative. He could get away from the Flying Y as soon as he could and keep going. His hope of seeing this thing through and some day getting the Lazy B back into his hands had faded to a mere flicker with Kerry's revelation that Clyde Carson was her cousin.

Light, coming from the lamp in its mirror bracket on the wall, flooded the big room opening off the porch. A long table was at the right of the room, and a big grandfather clock stood in the far corner. Across the room a bearskin rug covered the floor in front of the fireplace. Two chairs were there, and rising out of one of them was a tall gray-haired man who fixed his piercing steel-blue eyes on Blake.

Adam York had not changed much since the last time Blake had seen him. He still reminded Blake of a willow whip, dried out a little and stiffer, now, but resilient enough yet to spring back without breaking when bent.

"This Clyde?" York asked in the blunt manner that was typical of him.

35

Relief swept through Blake at the question. Obviously the old man did not know Carson.

"Yes, Pa," Kerry said. "Sheriff Ainsley tried to make him out a killer."

"A killer?" York exploded. "What's the matter with that harebrained idiot, anyway?"

"Don't blame the sheriff, Pa," Kerry said. "Clyde was a stranger. And somebody did kill Dan Blake out on the trail."

"Blake?" York exclaimed. "Son, if you killed him, you should get a medal."

"He didn't kill him," Kerry said. "You know Clyde is no killer."

"So Blake's dead." A grin broke across York's craggy face. "That's the best news I've heard for a while. Come on into my office, Clyde. I've got some things to talk over with you. Kerry can get supper while we're gabbing."

Kerry smiled at Blake and, turning, went on through the room into what Blake guessed to be the kitchen. He followed York into the little office, wondering how long he could keep up the deception.

York lit another lamp.

"Well, where's the money?" he demanded in his gruff, belligerent tone.

Blake had foreseen this question, and the answer called for more play acting. He lowered his gaze and shifted his weight. He said, "I had some trouble before I got to town."

"Trouble? What kind of trouble?"

"I was held up."

"You mean they got away with the ten thousand?" York shouted.

"That's what I mean, all right." Blake looked up as if scared of the old man. "If you can find fifty dollars on me, you're a magician. I knew I was heading into a rough country, but I didn't think it was this rough."

York began pacing the floor, his wrinkled face gray. Watching him, Blake felt a glow of triumph. This, in a small way, was striking back at the man who was responsible for his father's death.

Then Blake's mind turned to the young tenderfoot he had found along the trail. Here was ample reason for his death. The money Carson had been carrying had been enough to turn any drygulcher's gun on him, although Blake had no notion how the killer had known Carson had the money.

York wheeled to face Blake. "You see the men who held you up?"

"Masks are hard to see through," Blake said evasively.

"Didn't you see what they looked like?" York pressed. "Their build or the horses they were forking or anything?"

"Didn't notice the horses, but I think one of the men was short and wide and kind of squat."

"I knew it," York bellowed. "That sneaking back-shooting Joe Klitz. That's who it was. I told Ed Harms about the money I was expecting and he must have said something about it to Klitz. I never had the deadwood on that ornery son, but I've got it now."

"You can't prove anything," Blake said quickly. "I didn't get a look at any of their faces."

"You heard him talk, didn't you?" York demanded. "There isn't another voice in Nebraska like Joe Klitz's. You can identify him, all right. We'll ride into town first thing in the morning and get the sheriff. Then we'll fetch Klitz in and give him what he's got coming."

"You still won't get the money back," Blake said.

"I'll get the satisfaction of seeing Klitz behind bars." York began pacing again, worry shadowing his craggy face. "I don't know about the money, Clyde. I'll just have to stall Evans some more, but that isn't going to be easy. I've stalled him about as long as I can."

"Why not sell the Lazy B?" Blake asked speculatively.

"Sell it?" York shouted. "That outfit is part of the Flying Y and it's going to stay that way."

So Ben Evans had been wrong again. He had given Blake the idea that York would have to give up the Lazy B if things got tight enough. Obviously losing this ten thousand dollars was putting York in a real bind. But the old tyrant wasn't about to let the Lazy B go.

A cold rage gripped Blake as he watched the arrogant old man stride up and down the floor. There was some satisfaction in the fact that somebody had beaten York to the ten thousand dollars he had been counting on. That could lead to York's losing both spreads.

But if he did, they would go to Ben Evans. Maybe Blake would get the Lazy B from Evans. Maybe he wouldn't. Blake didn't trust the fat man.

York wheeled suddenly toward the door. "We'd better get washed up for supper. Then we'll get to bed. I reckon this has been a tough day for a pilgrim like you."

"A little tough," Blake admitted, and followed York out of the room.

He thought of the blunder he had made in giving even a vague description of one of the hold-up men. He didn't have the slightest idea who had held up Carson and taken York's money or what they looked like.

But he had been fully aware that he had to convince York or his game was up. He realized now that he had been thinking of the man in Ainsley's posse who had impressed him most when he had given his description to York. Ainsley had called that man Klitz.

This was putting Klitz in a tough spot. But Blake was in a tough spot of his own. The only thing he could do now was to ride this thing out. If he backed off, York would get suspicious.

CHAPTER
SIX

Adam York was an early riser, and he saw to it that those around him followed his example. So Blake garnered a nod of approval when he appeared for breakfast without being called.

York and Blake were on their way to town by the time the sun came up. It was a silent trip, York having little to say this morning and Blake welcoming the relief from probing questions. They rode without haste, although Blake had expected York to be burning with impatience.

"There's no all-fired hurry now," York explained as if reading Blake's thoughts. "If Klitz was aiming to run out with the money, he's long gone by now. If he isn't going to run, we can catch him just as well at noon as we can at ten o'clock."

The sun was two hours high when they rode into the main street of Winner. York suddenly pulled in at the hitchrack in front of Cruller's General Store, Blake following. As they dismounted, York pointed to three horses in front of the hotel.

"That's Klitz's outfit. I pay good money to those three loafers to run the Lazy B, and here they are in the hotel bar lapping up whiskey. If they see us ride up to the sheriff's office, they might get suspicious, so we'll walk over."

Nodding, Blake followed the old man up the street to the office of Sheriff Slinger Ainsley. They sauntered along unconcernedly until they reached the lawman's door, then stepped quickly inside and faced the surprised officer.

"What's on your mind, York?" Ainsley demanded, ruffling the papers on his desk in the manner of a busy man.

"I don't generally come in here to pass the time of day," York said testily. "I want to make an arrest."

Ainsley's papers became quiet. "Who and what's the charge?"

"Joe Klitz and his saddle bum pals, Reeves and Tarryall."

"But Klitz is working for you," Ainsley objected. "What's he done?"

"He's not working for me any more. He held up my nephew yesterday and robbed him. I want the money recovered, and I'm holding you responsible for the job."

"Now hold on." Ainsley rose and kicked back his chair. "I don't have any proof that Klitz held up this man." He glanced at Blake. "Can you identify Klitz as the bandit?"

"They were masked," York said sharply. "Even Klitz isn't fool enough to show his face on a job like that. You fetch him in and Clyde will identify him. I want the money, too."

"You don't want much," Ainsley said sarcastically. "If Klitz did rob your nephew, you can bet he's a long ways from here now."

"No, he's not," York snapped. "He's right over there in the Gold Bar. Now you get over there and arrest him."

Ainsley bristled. "Maybe you're the biggest rancher in these parts, but you're not big enough to tell me who I've got to arrest."

York pounded the desk. "You're sworn to uphold the law. You can't do it by crawling in a hole every time you smell trouble."

Ainsley reached for his hat. "Quit pawing the ground, you old mossyhorn. If it'll satisfy you, I'll go with you two over to the Gold Bar. We'll see what Klitz has to say about it."

"What do you think he'll say, you chuckle-headed idiot?" York bawled. "You think he'll start to cry and say he's sorry he did it? If Clyde identifies him, it'll be good enough for me."

"We'll see," Ainsley said, and stalked out of the office.

Blake followed Ainsley and York into the street and across to the hotel. It was a silent procession, York intent on cornering Klitz and neither Ainsley nor Blake anticipating the forthcoming encounter.

They crossed the lobby of the hotel and went through the door into the Gold Bar. The bartender was leaning idly on the mahogany, talking to his three early customers. As Ainsley's party came in, the barman looked up and broke off his recitation to the men across the polished counter from him. He stood motionless, staring, and the three others turned slowly to face those who had come in.

Blake forgot the bartender as he looked Klitz and the other two over. They had all been in the posse the day before. He remembered in particular the short, heavy-set man who was apparently the leader of the three.

"Looking for somebody, Sheriff?" the heavy-set man asked.

Blake knew then what York had meant when he'd said he would recognize Klitz's voice if he had ever heard it before. He had heard it yesterday when Klitz had verified the sheriff's assertion that the dead man they had brought in was Blake. At the time Blake had thought little about the voice, but now when Klitz spoke, the peculiar sandpapery quality of it struck him.

"York's doing the looking," Ainsley said.

Klitz swung to the rancher. "Looking for me?"

Ignoring Klitz, York motioned to Blake. "How about it, Clyde?"

"Hard to say," Blake said slowly. "They're about the same size, I reckon."

Klitz's face darkened. "What are you driving at?"

"Seems like our friend here was held up yesterday and relieved of some dinero," the sheriff said, jerking a thumb at Blake. "York has the idea that you staged the party."

"Me?" Klitz swung to face York, his hand hovering over the butt of his gun. "I don't take that from nobody."

"Easy now." Ainsley stepped forward, touching the gun at his side. "Nobody's guilty till he's proved that way."

"Arrest 'em," York demanded arrogantly. "All three of 'em. Clyde says they're about the size of the robbers."

"That's not good enough," Ainsley said flatly.

"Not good enough," York exploded. "Maybe Clyde should have noticed whether they had their fingernails cleaned or not."

"I've got to have some proof," Ainsley said. "All this tenderfoot nephew of yours has said is that they're about the size of the robbers. That's no proof at all."

York spun on his heel. "This country sure needs a sheriff with guts enough to arrest a man when he's guilty," he snapped as he strode out of the saloon.

Blake followed him, the sheriff a step behind.

They had reached the street when Blake was hailed from behind. "Hey, greenhorn."

Blake turned. Klitz was there, and in an ugly mood.

"What's wrong with you?" Blake demanded, irritated by the insolent tone Klitz had used.

"Nobody can go around saying I'm a thief and get away with it," Klitz shouted. "Not even a tenderfoot."

"I said you were about the size of one of the robbers," Blake said. "If the boot fits, wear it."

Klitz's black eyes blazed. "That's plenty, pilgrim, and then some!"

Klitz would have drawn if Ainsley had not grabbed his gun arm. "Hold it, Klitz. I'm not arresting you on York's charge, but if you start a rumpus now, I'll throw you into the jug as sure as you're a foot high."

Klitz hesitated, black eyes whipping from Blake to the sheriff and back. He said, "When anybody calls me a thief, he's got me to lick."

"Carson didn't accuse you," Ainsley said. "Forget it."

"You siding the greenhorn?" Klitz demanded.

"I'm keeping the peace," Ainsley retorted.

Klitz turned back to Blake, his face pulled into a scowl. "I'll settle with you, mister, and it'll be a time when you don't have the law to hide behind."

"I won't be hard to find," Blake said evenly.

Klitz turned back into the hotel. Shrugging, Blake caught up with York.

"I've got to see Ben," York explained. "Might as well come along."

York opened the door of Evans' private office and went in without the formality of knocking.

Evans looked up, scowling. "You might knock, Adam."

"I might," York admitted, "but I don't see any sense in wearing out my knuckles."

Evans pushed back his chair, his eyes touching Blake's face briefly, then swinging back to York's. "Sit down, Adam. What's on your mind?"

York dropped into a chair. "You can guess without straining your brain. You know I was aiming to pay you off with the money my nephew was fetching with him. Well, he got robbed yesterday before he got to town. Somebody knew he had the dinero, I reckon."

Evans leaned forward, fat hands on the desk top.

"Got any idea who it might have been?"

"Yeah, I've got an idea, but that worthless Ainsley won't do anything about it."

Blake was watching Evans closely, a new idea churning in his brain. York had just said Evans knew that Carson was coming with the money. It would be interesting, he thought, to know where Evans had been when Carson was robbed and killed.

"I'm sorry to hear that, Adam," the banker said. "I need that money and I need it bad."

"I suppose you'll take the Flying Y if I don't kick in right away," York said defiantly.

Evans spread his hands. "No use getting hot under the collar about it, Adam. It's cash I need most."

"Give me a little more time," York cried frantically. "I can raise it some way."

"All right," Evans said. "I'll let it go till the end of the month."

York glanced at the calendar on the wall. "You cross-eyed old rooster!" he shouted. "That's only four days. What do you think anybody can do in that time?"

"Don't call me a cross-eyed old rooster," Evans said ominously. "I've been giving you time, and all I've got is a bunch of promises. I've got to have the money by the end of the month."

"Or what?"

"Or I'll have to take over the Flying Y. Not that I want to, Adam, but I'm between a rock and a hard place myself. I borrowed some money from a bank in Omaha. Now they say I've got to show more security for my loans. You see how it is, Adam. It's you or me. And if I go under, the Omaha bank will take your note. They won't give you even four days."

York sat in silence, his head bowed.

"All right," he said at last, lifting his eyes to the banker's face. "Four days, and nothing to do but hope for a miracle. I've spent my life building up the Flying Y. It won't be easy just to walk out and leave it."

York rose, and the banker stood up with him. "I'm sorry, Adam," Evans said. "If anything turns up so I won't have to foreclose, I'll renew your note."

"I'm not licked yet," York said with sudden spirit. "Four days are enough to raise a considerable stink. Maybe I can raise some money along with it. I'm going to talk to Ainsley again." He turned to Blake. "Coming with me?"

"I'd like to talk to him for a minute," Evans said quickly. "I want to know more about that robbery."

"Hop to it," York said. "He told me all he knows. But you're welcome to talk his arm off if you want to." York stamped out of the office, slamming the door.

Blake waited until he heard the outside door of the bank slam shut; then he turned to face Ben Evans.

"Doesn't look like York is going to give up the Lazy B so easy," he said.

Evans sat down heavily. "The old fool is as stubborn as a mule on a cold morning. But you'll get the Lazy B one way or another. If York won't sell it to save the Flying Y, he'll lose them both."

"And you'll get them," Blake said.

Evans rubbed his fat hands together. "Right."

"Then do I get the Lazy B?"

"Oh, we'll work out a deal without any trouble."

"That wasn't the lay-out, Evans," Blake said ominously. "According to your letter, the Lazy B was practically mine for the taking."

"Now don't get riled," Evans said quickly. "I've got a lot of money wrapped up in those notes of York's, but I'll make it easy on you. In fact, if you'll string along with me till I get those ranches, I might just sign over the Lazy B to you scot free."

Blake studied the banker's face, sagging cheeks, thick lips, and small eyes. Not a face to trust.

"Just what will string along with you mean?" Blake asked, realizing that this was the thing Evans had wanted to talk to him about.

Evans leaned as far across the desk as his fat middle would allow. "I'll lay my cards right on the table, Blake. I need a fast gun to side me. Not that I expect to have to use it. Just having it should make it certain I won't need it."

"Think York will come gunning for you when you foreclose?"

"Maybe. But he's not the only one who might get trigger happy. How about it?"

Blake stood up. "Look, Evans, you don't want me. You want a man with a fast-gun reputation. To everybody around here, I'm a tenderfoot." He shook a finger at the banker. "You'd better remember that, too. I'm Clyde Carson from Ohio. If you get to thinking any different, you might have some fun explaining why you called me in to kill your 'good' friend, Ed Harms."

Evans waved his pudgy hands to quiet Blake. "I'm not forgetting a thing. But I saw you face Klitz a few minutes ago. You wear the gun brand, all right. If anybody crowds you, I figure you can show them."

"I don't aim to be crowded," Blake said. "And a tenderfoot's reputation isn't going to scare anybody."

"Well," Evans said, standing up, "I've made my offer. String along with me and the Lazy B will be yours."

"I'll think it over, Blake said, and went out of the office and across the bank lobby."

Outside the bank, he turned toward the sheriff's office to see if York was through arguing with Ainsley. But Hazel Thornton, coming up the boardwalk beside the bank, hailed him.

"I thought I saw you go into the bank with York a while ago," she said. "Thinking about settling in this country?"

Blake studied her face for a moment. "Hadn't thought too much about it. Any reason why I should?"

Hazel shrugged. "I'm just looking for prospects for our real estate business. If you get any ideas about wanting a piece of land anywhere around here, just drop into our office." She motioned behind her. "It's right in the back of the bank building, you know."

"So I heard," Blake said. "I'll keep you in mind if I decide to buy. Anything good on your docket now?"

"There are always good buys in a growing country like this. Ever take a look at the Lazy B Ranch?"

A chill ran through him. "I thought that belonged to York. Are you trying to see it?"

Hazel laughed. "We look for prospects for a piece of land, then try to buy it from the owner."

"And you think you can buy the Lazy B from York?"

Hazel's face became sober except for a little smile that tugged at the corner of her mouth. "Maybe. A person never knows what he can do until he tries."

"I'll look at the Lazy B sometime," Blake said, and went on down the street.

CHAPTER
SEVEN

It was almost sundown when Blake and York rode into the Flying Y yard. York had taken Blake past the Lazy B and shown him the lay-out. It had taken most of the afternoon.

"How would you like to run the Lazy B?" York asked suddenly.

Blake stared at York. This would be one way of getting back on the Lazy B. But it would be a far cry from owning it. And that was what he had come back here to do.

"It'll be a man-sized job," he said.

"That it will," York admitted. "But I figure you can do it."

"I won't have Klitz working for me," Blake said.

York nodded. "Your first job will be to fire him along with Reeves and Tarryall," he said blandly.

"What'll I do — run the outfit myself?"

"Of course not. You'll come to town day after tomorrow. I'll meet you in front of the hotel at noon with a new crew for you. You may have some trouble with Klitz. He won't take to the notion of being fired by a tenderfoot."

"That a warning?"

York puffed on his pipe a moment. "Just a caution. Don't give him a chance to use his gun. You'll probably have to work him over with your fists."

"You seem mighty sure I can handle him," Blake said irritably.

"If you're yellow, don't take the job," York snapped. "It'll be easier to back out now than when Klitz starts working on you."

"I'll go over in the morning."

Stealthily Kerry moved across the hall and rapped lightly on the door of the bedroom which Clyde was using. For a moment there was complete silence inside; then she heard someone moving around and a moment later the soft inquiry, "Who is it?"

"Kerry," she said softly. "I want to talk to you."

"Hold on a minute."

There was more shuffling around and the unmistakable thump of metal against wood. If it had been anybody but Clyde in there, she would have been sure that was a gun thumping against a wooden chair. But though Clyde wore a gun, surely he wouldn't grab it at the first sound of a visitor.

The door opened and she saw Clyde's face in the gloom. "Come in," he said.

She stepped inside. "I'm sorry if I got you out of bed, Clyde, but I had to talk to you."

"I wasn't asleep," he said. "I'll light the lamp."

"Don't bother. I'll only be here a minute, and I don't want Pa to know. He wouldn't like it if he knew I was talking against one of his plans."

"What plan do you mean?"

Her eyes were becoming accustomed to the darkness now, and she looked around the room before answering. On the back of the chair was Clyde's gun belt. Then she had heard right. He had reached for his gun at her knock. Her eyes whipped around to his face. What kind of a man was Clyde, anyway? Then she looked at the fancy trousers he evidently had pulled on quickly at her knock. Those weren't the clothes of a fighting man.

"Did Pa ask you to take over the Lazy B?"

"Why, yes, he did. How did you know?"

"I've talked to him about it. Clyde, you can't do that. Klitz is a killer."

"I can take care of myself."

"Not against Klitz. He is more dangerous than Pa realizes. I ride a lot, Clyde, and I see things I don't tell Pa because he wouldn't believe me. He trusted Ed Harms and Joe Klitz. But I think they were both selling him out. They're both cut from the same bolt of cloth."

"Didn't sound to me like your pa trusts Klitz."

"He doesn't now, and it hurts him to admit he made a mistake. But he used to trust Klitz completely. That's why he doesn't realize how vicious the man is."

"I can't back out now."

Kerry stamped her foot, suddenly angry. "Don't be a fool, Clyde. You're just afraid someone will think you're yellow, but that isn't worth getting yourself killed for. Klitz is the kind who will take any advantage he can get. That's the way he fights."

He touched her arm. "Why are you bothering to tell me this?"

She looked up at him quickly, startled at the tenderness of his touch. "Because you're my cousin, and it's not fair to let you go over there when you don't understand what you're riding into."

He backed off a step. "I think I know what's over there, Kerry. Stop worrying."

"I can't, Clyde." It was her turn to grip his arm, a spontaneous gesture. "I can't let you be murdered for nothing. You're the only relative who has ever come to see us that I've really liked."

He studied her face in the gloom, and she had the feeling he was looking right into her mind and reading her thoughts. "Whatever happens," he said finally, "it won't be your fault. So don't blame yourself."

"Then you're going to take the job, anyway?"

He nodded. "Yes."

Anger surged up in her. "You're just as pig-headed as all the other men I've known." She wheeled toward the door.

He caught her arm. "Wait, Kerry. I appreciate your telling me about Klitz. But I've got a job to do. It isn't just the way I'd planned it, but it will have to be this way."

"Of course," she snapped. "You're proud and conceited, like every other man. Well, I hope Klitz takes it out of you."

She jerked away from his hand and ran out, slamming the door behind her.

She thought of the chubby banker, Ben Evans. Surely he wouldn't foreclose unless it was absolutely necessary. She recalled the day not too long ago when she had been in the bank on an errand for her father and Evans had come out of his office to talk to her. He had assured her then that he would do everything possible to help the Yorks. He had urged her to come to him if she ever faced a problem she couldn't lick.

Well, she was facing one now. Maybe if she talked to Evans she could persuade him to extend the time just a few days. A few days could mean a lot when time was so short and the stakes were so high . . .

She slipped away from the ranch when it was barely light. She simply set the breakfast on the table for her father and Clyde, then went back into the kitchen as though for something she had forgotten and kept right on going through the kitchen door to the corral.

If her father found out what she had in mind, he'd put his foot down and not let her go. The only way was to be gone before he discovered she wasn't still in the kitchen. She was well on her way to town when the sun came up.

The bank wasn't open when Kerry got to Winner. She had to wait for Evans' teller to come and open the bank and then while away another half-hour before Evans himself arrived.

Ben Evans' face lost its morning gloom the minute he saw Kerry. His flabby features spread into a wide smile, and he motioned Kerry into his office beyond the lobby.

"If I'd known I was going to have such a pretty visitor this morning, I would have hurried down here," he said, finding a chair for Kerry and making certain she was seated comfortably.

"I had to see you, Mr. Evans," Kerry said. "Pa doesn't know I'm here. You told me once if I ever needed help to come to you. Well, I'm here."

Evans rubbed his hands together. "I'm glad you came to me. Now what do you need?"

"I think you know," Kerry said. "We have to have a little more time on our note."

Evans drummed his fingers on his desk. "I told your pa how it was."

Kerry left her chair and leaned over the desk. "Can't you extend it for just a few days?"

Evans smiled at her. "You make it mighty hard to refuse. But I'm in a bind, too." He continued to drum his fingers, scowling at them as though lost in deep thought. "I might be able to swing a few more days, Kerry, but it will take some doing."

"Thank you, Mr. Evans," Kerry said excitedly. "I'd do almost anything to help Pa pay off his loan."

"Now hold on," Evans said, holding up a hand. "I didn't say I could swing it. I said I might be able to. And you can do something to help."

"What?" Kerry asked eagerly.

Evans looked at her, eyes flashing. "You may think I've gone loco, but I haven't. I'm a lonely man, Kerry. If you could find it in your heart to look kindly on me —"

The strength went out of Kerry's legs and she staggered back to the chair and dropped into it. That was the last thing in the world she had expected from the banker.

Evans rose quickly and came around the desk. "I didn't mean to startle you. I've always thought you liked me. My intentions are purely honorable. I'm not such an old man, and I do have money. We could be happy together."

Kerry simply stared at him. Yet somehow it did not occur to her to mention that she was supposed to be engaged to Sid Saylor.

"What about Pa?" she heard herself say as though it came from someone completely detached from herself.

"Adam will see it our way. Don't worry. To get an extension on his loan, I'll have to work through an Omaha bank. It will be much easier if I know I really have something to work for. Don't you see, Kerry?"

Kerry got to her feet, her knees threatening not to cooperate. "I'll think it over, Mr. Evans. I just don't know."

"Of course," Evans said, his eyes sparkling like those of a cat with its eyes on a canary. "I want you to do what you want to do. But think about it carefully. Who else could give you things like you're used to? Remember, Adam York has given you the best. I can, too. And I might be able to keep the creditors off your pa's neck."

In a trance, Kerry walked out of Evans' office and mounted her horse.

CHAPTER
EIGHT

Dan Blake rode down the creek away from the Flying Y buildings just as the sun came up.

It was still early when he came into the Lazy B yard. He rode in the same way he had come three mornings before, but this time the crew was still here. He had expected that. They wouldn't be doing much work without a boss.

Smoke curled from the chimney of the house, but there was no other sign of life around the place. The horses were in the corral, apparently still without their morning feed. Blake pulled up at the hitchrail and dismounted. He loitered there a moment, but no one appeared. He was sure they were watching him, for they must have heard him ride in.

He tugged down the brim of his hat and strode to the house. Without ceremony he pulled open the screen door and walked into the big living room. The table was set for breakfast, but the three men were standing back, eyes on him as he entered.

"I didn't hear you knock," Klitz said softly.

"I don't knock when I come into my own house."

Klitz's brows lifted. "Your house?"

Blake nodded. "I'm taking over. York says I'm going to be the boss."

"Boss?" Surprise smothered the venom in Klitz's voice.

"That's right. Any objections?"

"Plenty," Klitz said angrily.

"What was York's idea," the lanky puncher called Tarryall demanded, "sending a tenderfoot over here to boss us?"

"Maybe I'm not as tender as you think," Blake said.

"And maybe you're not as tough as you think, either," Klitz sneered. "I'm bossing the outfit now that Ed Harms has cashed in."

"That's not what York says. I told him I'd ramrod the Lazy B, and that's what I aim to do."

"You're biting off a hunk of trouble," Klitz snapped.

"No reason for that," Blake said. "You're not even working here any more."

"What's that?" Klitz shouted. "Now you are talking mighty big, stranger."

"Carson is the name," Blake said. "You're fired as of right now. Start packing."

The flush deepened on Klitz's face. "It'll be a bigger hairpin than you to make that order stick," he said hotly.

"I'll make it stick, all right."

Klitz crouched a little, right hand hovering over his gun. "Start trying," he said.

Blake remained motionless for a moment, studying Klitz. Then he glanced at Tarryall and Reeves. They were standing back, confident of Klitz's ability to handle this tenderfoot who had the temerity to move in on them, but Blake wasn't fooled. They'd take a hand if they had to.

Carefully Blake unbuckled his gun belt. He felt suddenly naked as the Colt thumped to the floor. Maybe he was guessing wrong. If Klitz insisted on using a gun, Blake would never leave the room under his own power. With three against him, the odds were too heavy for guns, but there was a chance that Reeves and Tarryall would respect a fair fight with fists.

Blake was watching Klitz as he dropped his belt. "Get rid of that iron," he said. "I aim to fix your mug so it'll never look the same."

Surprise, then anger, flooded Klitz's face. With a muttered curse, he jerked open the buckle of his gun belt and let the belt fall. "Look's like you want it the hard way, bucko," he snarled. "I reckon you'll live to tell about it, but you'll wish you hadn't."

"Get outside, Joe," Reeves said. "More room."

Blake welcomed the change. He wanted plenty of room, for he didn't underestimate the strength of Klitz's short muscular arms. If Klitz ever got him cornered and secured a grip with those powerful arms, it would mean the end of the fight. And it would probably be Dan Blake's last fight with anyone.

Blake wheeled toward the door as he saw disappointment sweep over Klitz's face. Reeves' suggestion was not to Klitz's liking, for he could have used the close quarters of the room as an asset. Now he had little choice. He followed Blake into the bare yard, Reeves and Tarryall coming behind.

Blake had just stepped off the veranda when a grunt warned him of treachery at his back. He wheeled, jerking himself sideways, but the move wasn't quick enough to save him completely from the crushing weight of the stocky foreman.

Blake was knocked sprawling, but at an angle so that Klitz did not fall on him. The breath was jolted from him, but he rolled away quickly before Klitz could get his arms wrapped around him. He got to his feet, the air burning back into his lungs as Klitz climbed up, black rage in his face. Blake retreated, keeping out of reach of those powerful arms. He had been shaken by Klitz's sneak attack, and his movements were sluggish.

Klitz didn't wait for Blake to get set. He charged like an infuriated bull, and Blake sidestepped, driving in two quick blows that slowed the other man. But Klitz was not to be stopped by a few jolts. He kept driving in, and Blake stepped away, punching as he retreated. Then he reversed himself, stopping suddenly and driving two quick blows straight into Klitz's face, spinning him around and dropping him to one knee.

Reeves and Tarryall, watching in anticipation, suddenly howled as Klitz went down. They charged forward, and by the time Klitz had regained his feet, they were on Blake. Blake retreated again, knowing a moment of panic, for he was no match for the three of them.

Blake swung at Reeves, a precision blow to the point of the chin that knocked the short puncher flat. There were only two then, but while he held his own with Klitz, the angular Tarryall was landing blows that hurt.

60

He had guessed wrong in thinking that Reeves and Tarryall would honor a fair fight, and he was paying for that wrong guess.

Blake stepped inside one of Tarryall's long-armed jabs and planted a hard fist on the tall puncher's slanting nose, but at the same time he left himself open for a stunning blow that Klitz exploded on his ear. Then into his dimmed vision came Reeves, shaking his head, charging in to get even for the punch that had put him out of the fight momentarily.

Now Blake found himself backed against the hitchrail, Klitz in front of him, Reeves and Tarryall blocking either side. He was trapped, and he knew it. Sheer weight would put him down.

But before the three could move in for the finish, a gun roared and dust spurted up behind Klitz. The fight stopped abruptly.

"Kind of short-handed, aren't you, Joe?" a girl asked.

Blake looked up, bringing a sleeve across his sweaty, blood-smeared face. The girl was Hazel Thornton, riding a chestnut mare, leaning nonchalantly on the saddle horn, a .32 balanced in her hand. There was a trace of a smile on her lips as she looked at the men.

"We were taking care of things all right," Klitz said angrily. "Fancy-pants here allows he's running the place. He figured to fire us, so we were showing him who was boss."

"Couldn't you do it yourself?" Hazel asked contemptuously.

"Sure," Klitz snapped. "I didn't invite the boys in."

"Then I'll invite them out again." She motioned with the barrel of her gun to Reeves and Tarryall. "Get back. Let Joe stomp his own snake."

"I'm not taking orders from any tenderfoot," Reeves said darkly.

"Joe will take care of that," Hazel said.

"And I'm not taking any orders from a woman, either," Tarryall snapped. The tall puncher started toward Blake but stopped almost immediately.

"You will this time, Jim." The gun in Hazel's hand tilted ominously. "Stay back, or I'll blow out what few brains you do have."

The grumbling Tarryall stepped back to stand beside Reeves. Klitz glared at Hazel.

"Have you gone plum loco?" he demanded.

"Hadn't noticed it," Hazel said. She looked at Reeves and Tarryall, then brought her eyes back to Klitz. "Now, my tough friend, let's see who fires who." She dropped her left hand to the saddle horn, her right hand still gripping the gun.

If Blake had any doubts about whether or not the fight would be resumed, they were gone the next instant as Klitz launched himself forward in an attempt to catch Blake off guard again. Blake spun away from the hitchrack and, getting good ground under him, opened a cold waiting campaign.

Klitz had been hurt, but he was a powerful man. Now he rushed, intent on finishing Blake as soon as possible. Blake parried Klitz's blows, taking them on his elbows and arms or turning a shoulder, and all the time he was punching his left fist into Klitz's face, stinging blows that added to the big man's fury.

Then Klitz connected with Blake's cheek. Blake fell back, apparently half stunned, and Klitz came in fast, fists flying, his guard down. It was exactly the situation Blake had been working for. He suddenly straightened and exploded with a counterattack. Surprise weakened Klitz as he fell back, pawing wildly in a futile attempt to block Blake's blows.

Blake landed a solid right to Klitz's nose that brought a shower of blood, but he kept trying for the big man's jaw. Twice he got his right through, but each time Klitz fell back and the blows lacked knockout force.

Then Blake drove a fist into Klitz's stomach that brought the air out of his lungs in an audible gasp. As he bent forward, his jaw exposed, Blake swung with his right and connected solidly. Klitz went down, stumbling and sprawling headlong into the boot-trodden earth of the yard.

Blake leaned against the hitch pole, panting, feet wide apart, one hand wiping blood from the corner of his mouth. There was no sound for a moment except the heavy breathing of Reeves and Tarryall.

"Does that settle who's going to boss this outfit?" Blake asked.

"It should," the girl said. "What about it, boys? You want to try your luck one at a time?"

"Not me," Tarryall said. "Come on, Bud."

Tarryall turned into the house, Reeves at his heels.

"Don't forget to pack Klitz's stuff, too," Blake called.

"Where's your gun?" Hazel Thornton asked.

Blake wiped his mouth again with the back of his hand. "My gun's inside. I took it off."

"You're not very smart," she said scornfully, "or you'd never take your gun off when you're up against a man like Klitz."

"I'm not so sure," Blake said. "Maybe I wanted to live a little longer. I couldn't gun down all three of them."

Klitz stirred and slowly got to his feet. He stumbled into the house, head bowed, a bruised and badly beaten man. He came out presently, following Reeves and Tarryall, his bedroll over his shoulder. The three went to the corrals and saddled up. They mounted and rode out of the yard, Klitz glaring at Blake from his one good eye. The other was black and swollen shut. With a touch of spurs the three thundered out of sight.

Blake turned back, looking at the girl.

"Come in," Blake said, jerking his head toward the house.

The girl shook her head. "I've got some riding to do. I've lost enough time now. Just tell me one thing and I'll be going."

Something in her voice warned him. "What do you want to know?" he asked.

"Who are you?"

"Clyde Carson," he said evenly, not letting his set countenance show the shock that raced through him.

She nodded. "I heard that before, but it doesn't go with me. I've been East. I've seen men fight back there, nice men who knew the rules. You didn't learn your brand of fighting in Ohio."

"I've been out here before," Blake said.

She shrugged, smiling. "Maybe. Well, I'm not one to argue. You can handle your fists. I've seen that much. Now I'll tell you something. You're too good a scrapper to be on the losing side. How would you like to deal yourself in on something good?"

"I've got something good."

She laughed. "Mister, you don't know good from bad. You're working for York, and he's a dead duck. If you stick with him, you can't win."

"Have you got any stake in seeing York go under?"

She studied his face for a moment. "Maybe. Maybe not. The day of men like Adam York is gone. We're coming into a new age. You and I belong to that age. I've got to ride now. But I want to talk over a proposition with you. Can you find that old soddy on the slough between here and the Flying Y?"

Blake nodded. He had seen the soddy that morning on his ride over to the Lazy B. It had looked pretty dilapidated to him. "I know where it is."

"Meet me there at four this afternoon," Hazel said.

"Maybe I'll be busy around the ranch here."

She flipped her quirt idly across her gloved hand. "Are you afraid of me or the proposition I may make to you?"

He met her steady gaze. "I never saw the girl or the proposition I couldn't turn down."

She laughed. "I like you, Mr. Carson, or whoever you are. I'll see you at the soddy at four. And by the way, wear your gun. You look undressed without it."

He started to go into the house but stopped as he caught the sound of hoofbeats. His first thought was that Klitz and his two pals were coming back to finish the job Hazel had kept them from doing before. He ran toward the house to get his gun. Then, halfway there, he realized only one horse was coming in. And it was coming from the opposite direction from that which Klitz and Hazel had taken. They had both headed toward town.

He turned to look at his visitor while the rider was still beyond the corrals and recognized Dr. Gentry. There was no mistaking that stooped figure, although Blake had never seen him on a horse before. He waited until Gentry rode into the yard and reined up in front of him.

"Get down, Doc," Blake invited. "Come in and rest a spell."

"No time," Gentry said, "unless you need some doctoring on those bruises."

"I'll make out," Blake said, dabbing at the blood at the corner of his mouth where it was beginning to dry.

"What did Hazel want here?" Gentry asked bluntly.

"I'm not sure," Blake said. "She said something about a business proposition. I was glad to see her, regardless. If she hadn't stepped in, I'd have been in real trouble with those three men I fired."

Gentry nodded as though not hearing half that Blake had said. "A business proposition," he said thoughtfully. "It is wise to consider all propositions carefully. Thank you, Mr. Carson."

Blake watched Gentry rein his horse into the road leading toward town. The man's visit completely mystified him.

CHAPTER
NINE

Bruce Gentry was slumped in a chair in his office when the back door of the office opened and the banker, Ben Evans, came in.

"I thought I saw you ride in," Evans said. "Where have you been?"

"Riding," Gentry said.

"Riding where?" Evans moved around to face Gentry, his beady eyes pinned on the doctor's face.

"What difference does it make? You don't own me body and soul."

"Oh, don't I?" Evans paced the floor excitedly. "Listen, Gentry, you know why I brought you here and set you up in business."

Gentry grunted. "You call this a business?"

"It is so far as the town is concerned. You stay in your office during office hours unless I tell you to leave."

A spark of resistance flickered in Gentry's eyes. "And if I don't?"

"You wouldn't want anything to happen to Hazel, I know. Keep that in mind."

Gentry sank back in his chair. How could one man hate anybody as much as he hated Ben Evans and still live? Yet he wasn't man enough to do anything about it. He hadn't been able to do anything about it twelve years ago when Evans, an obscure bank clerk and a distant cousin of Gentry's, had come to Chicago for a week's visit and had been a house guest at Dr. Gentry's suburban home.

In that week, while Dr. Gentry tended to the ills of his patients, Ben Evans had won the affections of Flossie Gentry, a nervous, flighty woman but one whose loyalty Bruce Gentry had never questioned.

It had been a trumped-up deal from the very first. Gentry had never suspected when Ben Evans thanked him for his week's hospitality and left. And he didn't suspect the young woman patient who began coming to him soon after that. He never could find anything physically wrong with the woman.

He hadn't seen the trap until it was sprung. That had been the night when he had been called to the home of this young woman on the pretense that she was very ill. They had barged in while he was trying to find what was wrong with the woman. There had been his wife, Flossie, Ben Evans, and two others who were called later as witnesses.

It was enough so that practically everything Bruce Gentry owned was awarded to his wife when she got her divorce. Two weeks after the divorce she married Ben Evans. She had died just a few months after that. But it had left Ben Evans in control of the small fortune young Dr. Bruce Gentry had accumulated in his short but brilliant career.

Bruce Gentry hadn't seen the trap when it had been set for him. But he had seen the power behind it once his eyes were opened. Ben Evans' planning had been responsible for the whole thing. It hadn't been enough that he take Gentry's wife; he had wanted his fortune, too. And he had gotten it. With it, he had opened his bank here in Winner and was trying to accumulate a bigger fortune.

Looking at the fat man now, Gentry hated himself for allowing the man to use him as he was doing. For Gentry knew that somehow Evans was using him to make certain he gained control of this entire country. Hazel was the key, but as yet Evans hadn't revealed how he was going to use that key.

"Hazel isn't like me, Ben," Gentry said. "She can take care of herself."

Evans shrugged. "Up to a certain point. But I can go beyond that point. Don't forget that."

Gentry rose from his chair, facing Evans. "Some day I'll kill you, Ben," he said, breathing heavily.

Evans grunted. "You couldn't kill a fly. You're put together wrong."

"A man can stand only so much."

"You can stand more. I brought you here so you could be close to your daughter. But if you don't do as I tell you, you'll end up going to her funeral."

Evans wheeled and went out the back door of the office as he had come. Gentry stared at the closed door for a minute after Evans was gone.

When his wife had left him over a decade before, she had left their daughter with him.

Then when she was eighteen, Hazel had left home. He had heard from her only once after that when she wrote to him, telling him she had changed her name and that he wouldn't hear from her again. She was going to get a fresh start.

It wasn't until then that he fully realized how much she blamed him. He had always thought she blamed her mother. But she blamed him for not fighting for what was rightfully his. And by then it was too late.

For six years then he had wandered aimlessly, almost forgetting his medical practice. Then he had been traced down by Ben Evans and told that if he came to Winner, he could be close to Hazel again. Not only that; Ben Evans would set him up with a respectable practice.

He should have known better than to take anything from Ben Evans. A skunk's stripe might be changed with whitewash but the smell couldn't be eliminated. Ben Evans and his schemes still smelled.

Now Gentry was here and he had seen Hazel. But she wanted nothing to do with him. It hadn't taken him long to see that she and the man she was with, George Thornton, were up to their eyes in some shady scheme. And Evans was either in it with them or wished he was and was trying to out-swindle them.

Gentry moved around the office nervously. It wasn't in him to sit idly when his mind was in such a turmoil, and he waited for patients that never came.

Half an hour after Evans left, Gentry opened the back door and looked over the alley. Nothing was stirring. The door that opened out of Ben Evan's office into the alley was closed. The door into Thornton's office was around on the other side.

Getting his hat, Gentry slipped out the door into the alley. There was no stir anywhere as he went along the back of the bank to Thornton's office. Hazel would surely be there now.

But when he went in, only George Thornton was there. Thornton looked up, the pleasant smile on his face chilling to a dark scowl.

"What do you want, Gentry?"

"I want to see Hazel."

"She isn't here now. Anyway, she doesn't want anything to do with you."

Gentry dropped into a chair. "I'll let her tell me that."

"She will," Thornton said. He got up from his desk. "Now get out of here. Somebody might come in."

"I won't hold the door so they can't," Gentry said.

Thornton came around to stand in front of Gentry's chair. "Hazel told me all about you: how you wouldn't fight for anything that belonged to you. Now you've come to town just when we were doing all right and you've messed up everything. So get out of my office and stay out!"

Thornton grabbed Gentry by the back of the shirt and lifted him out of the chair. A strange defiance surged through Gentry. He had had about all the pushing he could take for one day. He swung an elbow around and caught Thornton in the stomach.

Breath hissed out of Thornton and he bent over, releasing his grip on Gentry. But the next instant he straightened up and swung a fist that caught Gentry on the side of the head.

Gentry felt himself hurtling through the air before he crashed into the desk. He didn't lose consciousness, but all the fight in him evaporated and he slumped against the desk, not trying to get up.

He saw Hazel come through the door just then. For a moment she stared at him and at Thornton; then she took three quick steps that brought her face to face with Thornton.

Gentry tried not to listen to the things Hazel said to Thornton. But he caught the main theme of her tirade, and he almost smiled when Thornton grabbed his hat and slammed out of the office.

Hazel turned to him and held out a hand to help him to his feet. "What's the idea of coming here?" she demanded, no gentleness in her voice.

"I wanted to talk to you, Hazel," he said, going back to the chair and dropping in it.

"There's nothing for us to talk about now. You had six years to talk to me when it would have done some good. You wouldn't do anything then. You can't do anything now."

"You're mixing into bad business, Hazel," Gentry said. "Evans is tricky, the scum of the earth."

Hazel slapped the quirt dangling from her wrist against the leg of her riding pants. "There's nothing you can tell me about Ben Evans. Why do you think George and I came here to this flea-bitten town? To get from Ben Evans what is coming to me, that's why."

"He stole your money and your property just as surely as if he'd held you up with a gun. I'd have had that money now as your daughter if you'd had backbone enough to go after it. Well, you didn't have, but I do. George and I are going to get every penny Ben Evans has!"

Gentry sat motionless, only his eyes following Hazel's restless pacing. Could this be the daughter he had sired? This was a hard, unyielding woman. That gun she wore like a man wasn't just a showpiece.

"What about this Thornton you're living with? That isn't right."

"George Thornton is a perfect partner for me," Hazel said. "He's smart enough to outwit most men and he can outfight any he can't. And don't be shocked. We're living together as man and daughter, not as man and wife. He's more of a father to me than you are."

Gentry winced.

"Why don't you leave the country, Pa?" Hazel said, suddenly stopping in front of Gentry's chair. "Before you came, George and I had things going pretty much our own way. I'm soft-headed enough to try to keep you in one piece. And it's messing up our whole plan."

"You think you know Ben Evans," Gentry said. "But you don't. He's more treacherous than any snake you ever saw. I've got to stay to protect you from him."

Amazement spread over Hazel's face. "You protect me?" she exclaimed. "That's the biggest joke I've heard in a month. I can take care of myself."

"That's why I'm staying, Hazel. You think you can take care of yourself. I know you can't."

74

After staring at Gentry for a long minute in disbelief and disgust, Hazel spun on her heel. "I've got to see George on some important business and I don't have much time. I've got an appointment at four this afternoon."

She walked out of the office as though she were the visitor instead of he. Gentry watched her go, feeling more helpless than ever.

CHAPTER
TEN

When Dan Blake left the Lazy B at three-thirty that afternoon for his four o'clock appointment with Hazel Thornton he rode with caution. Something about this whole thing didn't add up.

The slough where he was headed was only a couple of miles from the Lazy B so Blake rode slowly. He didn't want to get there much ahead of time; just enough to look the situation over carefully before riding up to the old soddy.

He saw no stir around the soddy when he first came in sight of it. But as he circled it, he saw a horse standing along the south wall, out of sight of any rider on the trail to the north.

Reining into the slough, he let his horse splash through the shallow water and sucking mud, climb the bank a hundred yards from the soddy. There he reined up for a moment. If there was a trap set for him, it should show itself now.

But Hazel came out of the soddy and motioned for him to come on. He nudged his horse forward. He had nothing to fear from Hazel; at least, not until she was sure just where he stood. But that horse could have belonged to Klitz or Reeves or Tarryall.

"Right on time, I see," Hazel said when he reined up and dismounted. "Better put your horse on the south side of the house with mine. No sense in advertising our meeting here."

"Expecting somebody to ride by?"

Hazel shook her head. "It's the fellow who prepares for the unexpected who survives."

"Can't argue with that." He led his horse around the corner of the soddy, then came back to stand beside Hazel, who was staring dreamily out over the slough.

"Sort of pretty in a way, don't you think?" she said.

He let his eyes run over the slough, turning green now.

"Sure, it's pretty," he said. "I like the hills, too, and the flat land in the spring."

"You sound as if you'd been here before."

He caught himself and turned to meet her suspicious eyes. "A fellow doesn't have to be here long to see the beauty of the land."

"How about the blizzards in the winter?"

Blake grinned. "Winters in Ohio are different from those they have here, if what they say about this country is true."

She moved closer to him. "How about the springs? You can compare them."

He studied her upturned face. She wasn't interested in the seasons here or in Ohio. Just what was she interested in?

"What about the proposition you were going to make me?" he asked.

"Oh, business," she said disgustedly. "Can't we forget it for a little while? I'd like to relax and just talk for a few minutes."

She moved closer to him, and he tried to analyze this sudden show of affection.

Suddenly Hazel stopped, her eyes growing wide as she stared at something on the ground behind Blake. She stifled a scream.

"Snake! Snake!" she cried, pointing behind him.

He wheeled, his gun coming into his hand as he moved. He saw it, less than ten feet from him, head cocked above the grass. He fired almost before he stopped turning, the bullet slapping its target and knocking it spinning into the grass several feet away.

For a moment all was quiet; then Hazel moved around Blake. "That was my quirt," she said apologetically, and went over to pick it up. "You really made a mess of it." She held up the quirt, showing where the bullet had slapped into the braided leather.

He remembered how the quirt had looked in that split-second before he shot, as much like a snake as a piece of leather could.

"How did your quirt get down there?" he asked.

"Must have dropped it."

He knew then. There wasn't one chance in a thousand that a dropped quirt could land and lie as this one had. It had been planted. And he knew why. Hazel had wanted to see him handle a gun. She hadn't believed he was a tenderfoot.

Hazel slipped the quirt onto her waist again and came toward him, slapping the leather gently against her leg. "You know, Mr. Carson, for a greenhorn, you handle that gun pretty well."

"I told you I'd been out here before. A man has to learn some things fast to survive out here."

"I've seen men survive out here who never had their hands on a gun. I doubt if Dr. Gentry is a good hand with a gun."

"Probably not," Blake said.

"You must learn mighty fast. I've known men who have handled guns all their lives who aren't half as good as you are."

"Maybe you don't understand how fast I catch onto things," Blake said.

She laughed. "Maybe not. But where you're from or how fast you learned that draw isn't important. What is important is that you've got the qualifications for the job I had in mind."

"And what job is that?"

"I would rather you came in and talked it over with Dad. He's the one who handles all the business."

"Oh?" Blake studied her face. "I had the impression that you made the decisions."

She laughed. "Don't let Dad hear that. What he doesn't know won't hurt him, you know."

"I'd like to know something about the kind of a job you'd have for a tenderfoot like me."

"It's not the tenderfoot we want. It's the man who wears the gun brand. You wear the brand, all right; clothes can't hide that. I thought so when I saw that you tied down your holster. Nobody but a gunman needs do that."

He considered arguing but thought better of it. Nothing he could say now would change Hazel's mind about him. She had seen him draw and fire. That was enough to stamp the gun brand on him. And as far as she was concerned, it would stick.

"You will come in tomorrow morning and talk to Dad, won't you?" Hazel pressed when Blake kept quiet too long.

Blake shrugged. "No harm in talking, I guess. But remember, I've got a ranch to run."

"For York," Hazel said disgustedly. "But running the ranch won't interfere with the job we have for you."

Hazel went around the soddy and got her horse, swinging astride like a man.

"See you at the office in the morning," she called as she spurred her horse into a gallop toward town.

Blake watched her go, more puzzled than ever about her.

He didn't go directly back to the Lazy B headquarters. He angled up on the bluff that overlooked Prairie Creek and rode along the rim of hills that shunted the creek out onto the flat land. From one of the highest hills, he could see the town of Winner, a little splotch on the horizon. The sinking sun reflected from a tin roof somewhere in town and flashed a spear of light in Blake's eyes.

Closer to him he could see the squat sod houses of homesteaders between the town and the river. A few abandoned soddies were along the creek itself, houses that Adam York had made certain never became homes.

Blake reined his horse on to the east. He had a reason for staying up on the bluff. He had a place to visit before riding down to the ranch buildings.

It was sundown when he reached the little ten-foot-square lot on the highest hill overlooking the Lazy B buildings. It was fenced in with three strands of barbed wire. In the center of the lot was a grave, barely recognizable as such now. Weeds and grass had overgrown it and the mound had sunk away, but the fence had stood against weather and wandering animals.

When that grave had been put there, Dan Blake had sworn he would come back and settle with the ones who had been responsible. Harms was dead now. But the job was only half done.

It seemed like treason to be working for Adam York. Yet he could probably never find a better way to strike at York than to work for him as Ed Harms had worked for Jim Blake. The time would come when Dan Blake could give York a dose of his own medicine.

It was dark when Blake left the grave and let his horse pick his way down the steep slope to the corral. His thoughts were still wandering back through the years when his father had owned the Lazy B and he was a green kid just learning the ropes.

Then, just as he reached the corral gate, he was suddenly jolted into the present as his horse threw up its head and whinnied.

Blake slid out of the saddle and stood waiting, his mind racing. His horse had caught the scent of an equine brother and had whinnied a welcome.

Ordinarily that would have been no cause for alarm, for there should be horses in the corral. But this morning Blake had turned the remaining horses out to pasture after Klitz and his men had taken theirs. Unless those horses had come back, which wasn't likely, there shouldn't be another horse within a mile of these buildings.

Blake slipped his gun into his hand as he stepped softly around in front of his horse and slid back the corral bars. In the dim light he saw that the corral was empty. Either the visiting horse was in the barn or around the house. Neither boded any good for Blake.

He let his horse into the corral but didn't stop to unsaddle him. Turning the animal loose, he crouched down beside the corral and waited. The horse trotted around the corral, finally stopping close to the barn and whinnying again.

Blake moved noiselessly along the corral fence, keeping low. Whoever was there had put his horse in the barn. Maybe he was with his horse or maybe he was in the house waiting. Blake was gambling that he was in the barn. If someone hadn't been there to keep the horse quiet, there would have been an answering nicker.

Then, halfway to the barn, Blake paused. A figure had appeared in the barn doorway. He took a step toward the horse in the corral, and Blake saw that he held a gun. He considered shooting first and asking questions later, for the man obviously was there for no good. But it wasn't in Blake to gun a man down without giving him a chance.

He started to stand up to call for the man to drop his gun when the man turned toward the barn door.

"He didn't even unsaddle him," the man said so softly Blake barely made out the words.

Blake settled down again. He had more than one visitor. If he had called out to this fellow, it would have been a fatal move. Someone inside the barn would have cut him down.

Then suddenly a shot rang out and a splinter ripped from the pole a few inches from Blake's head. He wheeled. That shot hadn't come from the barn; it had been fired from the house. He was caught like a sitting duck between the two.

Another flash came from the house, but the bullet was wider than the first. It was too dark for accurate shooting. Blake realized what his chances would have been if he'd ridden straight in without stopping at the grave overlooking the ranch. Whoever was laying for him had been there before dark. Their ambush, using both house and barn, was testimony to that.

The guns in the barn opened up then, but they had no clear target to shoot at. It was the gun at the house that worried Blake. He was on the house side of the corral fence.

Ducking low, he ran back toward the gate, bullets from the house probing the dusk for him. Just inside the corral and to one side of the gate was the watering trough. When Blake got even with the trough, he rose up and vaulted over the fence, getting a sliver in his hand but staying in the air only a second. Bullets snapped past in the darkness, but none hit him.

Then he was inside the corral, the fence between him and the house, the watering trough between him and the barn. He watched for the flashes as the guns in the barn tried to seek out his hiding place.

He fired at the flashes, concentrating on the guns in the barn. They were much closer than the one at the house. He wasn't sure he was even coming close, but at least it was a stand-off.

He became aware suddenly that the shooting from the house had stopped. Glancing back that way, he saw the man running in a low crouch toward the corral. The man obviously expected the guns in the barn to keep Blake too busy to notice him until he got close enough for an accurate shot between the corral poles.

Blake waited until the man was within twenty yards, then fired twice. The man staggered and went down. Blake couldn't wait to see how effective his shots had been. He wheeled back and sent two quick shots into the barn doorway.

The shooting from the barn, which had been almost continuous while the man from the house had been running in on Blake, now stopped. Blake could hear water spurting out of the trough on the other side where bullets had pierced the wood. It was running back under the trough, and Blake found himself crouching in an inch of mud and water.

Blake reloaded his gun, wondering what the strategy of the drygulchers in the barn would be now. The sudden drum of hoofbeats was his answer.

Rising from his hiding place, Blake ran toward the barn, zigzagging his way in a low crouch. This could be a trick. One man might have ridden out while the other waited, or they might even have sent a riderless horse galloping away to draw him out from behind the trough.

But he reached the barn without a shot being fired. Whoever had been in the barn had apparently seen his partner go down and decided he had had enough for one night.

Blake went through the barn, then lighted the lantern. Two heaps of empty cartridges, one at the door, one at the window, told the story. Two men had been there, and apparently only one had been in the house. They would have been the three men he had fired from the Lazy B that morning. He hadn't expected Klitz to strike back so soon or from ambush.

Blake went back to the man who had fallen twenty yards outside the corral. It was Reeves. That meant Klitz and Tarryall had been the two who had been in the barn. They would still have to be reckoned with, especially Klitz.

He went on into the house. He'd have no more trouble tonight, he was certain. Tomorrow when he went into town, he'd tell Dr. Gentry and he could send somebody out for Reeves.

Blake was tired. It had been a hard day, and tomorrow promised to be no easier.

CHAPTER
ELEVEN

Blake was in Winner an hour before noon. Noon was the time Adam York had set for delivering the new crew. But Blake wanted to see George Thornton before he met York.

He reined in at the hitchrack in front of the bank. Flipping the reins around the bar, he went up the street to Dr. Gentry's office and told the doctor about Reeves. He'd explain to Ainsley later if he had time. Going back outside, he walked past the door of the bank and along the side of the building.

He found a door at the back of the building with a window close by. Looking through the window, he saw George Thornton seated at a small desk. Hazel was standing beside him, saying something to him.

Blake knocked. After a moment of silence, a loud "Come in" ushered him inside.

Thornton stood up. "Glad to see you, Carson. Come in and have a chair. Hazel said you'd be in today."

Blake glanced at the girl. "What else did she say?"

Thornton grinned and sat down. "She talks quite a bit. And some of the things she says make very good listening."

Blake sat down gingerly, his eyes moving from Thornton to Hazel and back. "She hinted a lot yesterday," he said. "But she didn't say anything. I take it you're ready to tell me something now."

"She wanted to be sure about you. Carson. We need a man, a certain kind of man. We think you're it."

Blake nodded. "A man wearing the gun brand?"

"Exactly." Thornton hunched forward in his chair. "And also a man with vision. What we're planning to do isn't going to be accomplished in a day. I want men around me who can see far enough into the future to stay with me even if the going gets rough. We're undertaking something revolutionary. That's why we're going out of our way to attract men who possess vision and understanding."

"Strikes me you're looking for trouble," Blake said bluntly, "and you're trying to sign up some fighting men."

Thornton smiled. "You're a discerning man, Mr. Carson. I'll be frank about this. We'll have opposition. There always is, you know, when new people come to a community and start a progressive project."

"If you need gunslingers," Blake said, "I don't fill the bill."

Thornton's smile remained fixed on his lips. "I'm satisfied with the report I have on you. Hazel says you can handle your fists, too."

"Look, Thornton, you're just chasing this rabbit all over the country. You didn't invite me in here because I whipped a man."

"You're right," Thornton agreed. "There is another reason. You can be of help to our project along Prairie Creek."

"What's Prairie Creek got to do with your business here?"

"Everything, Carson. I'm a civil engineer. My daughter and I are interested in a project that will increase the value of this country hundreds of times."

Suddenly it struck Blake. "Irrigation," he said, the word bursting out of him.

It might do exactly what Thornton had said, or it might be a blight on the country, depending on how it was managed. Blake, looking at the man who proposed to do the managing, wasn't sure whether it would be a blessing or a curse.

"That's right," Thornton said affably: "Irrigation. The land north of the river is good. All it lacks is water. With plenty of water, there is no limit to what it could produce."

"Have you told the farmers around here?"

"Of course not. No point in getting their hopes up till we know what can be done."

"Just what does all this mean to me? I'm no ditch digger."

Thornton laughed softly. "I'm not looking for ditch diggers yet. When I start, I won't be after men like you who can swing a fist or a gun better than a pick. But if you stick with me, I stand ready to deal you in on the profits."

"Where do the profits come in?"

"When we get the dam in, we'll lay out a ditch system, then sell the land to the farmers coming in. I tell you there's a fortune in it."

"Who'll make the fortune, the farmers or us?"

"In time the farmers will make it. We'll make ours now."

"The ranchers aren't going to take this lying down. You know what York has done to the settlers along Prairie Creek."

"It's like I said. There is always opposition to progress."

Blake took a deep breath. "And I'm supposed to ride herd on your ditch diggers to see that no rancher uses them for target practice."

Thornton shot a glance across at Hazel. "That's guessing pretty close. There will be trouble, I'm afraid, in spite of our best efforts."

"Just what land are you going to irrigate? York owns most of the land along the creek."

"He claims it, but he doesn't own it. I don't know how you're going to take this, being York's nephew. But I'm going to lay it on the line. York is finished as a big cattleman. He may not know it but he's done."

He tried to grab all the land along the creek and run out the settlers. But he hasn't done it. In fact, we're going to build the dam on land still owned by a homesteader."

Blake studied Thornton closely. Somehow Thornton didn't sound enthusiastic enough to be convincing. Just how far did he plan to go with this project? And if not all the way, why was he starting it at all?

And why did he want to hire a gun to back him?

"Putting in a dam won't get you any land to irrigate," Blake said.

"I know it. But York's going under and I'm going to grab the river land when he does."

"You know about Evans pushing York into a corner?"

Thornton nodded. "Sure. But I've got a better idea than that. It will even give York a way out."

Blake shifted in his chair. "Meaning what?"

"I'll take over York's debt to Evans and pay him a profit besides."

Blake laughed. "You ought to know Adam York better than that. He's so bull-headed he won't give an inch until he's down and hog-tied."

"Being his nephew, surely you can talk to him," Thornton said. "He's not a stupid man, Carson. Show him that it's better to take a little than to get nothing."

Blake saw that Thornton was in earnest.

"Nobody shows the old man anything," Black said. "If that's what you called me in here for — to talk York into selling to you — you've just wasted your time."

"That was the easy way," Thornton said. "It's not the only way. Either way I'd like to put you on my pay roll."

Blake hesitated. He wanted to smash York as badly as Thornton did, but for different reasons.

"I'll think about it," Blake said. "I'm new here. I want to know just which way the wind is blowing before I start my fire."

"Time's pretty short," Thornton said. "York's got only another day or two. It will be to your advantage to string along with me."

"When I'm sure of that, I'll play along," Blake said.

He got up and headed for the door, feeling the eyes of Thornton and Hazel on his back.

He stepped outside the office and shut the door. There he stopped, watching the man hurrying toward him from the front of the bank.

"Joe's looking for you, Carson," Jim Tarryall said, stopping twenty feet from Blake.

"Then why doesn't he come after me instead of sending you?"

"I don't mind running his errands," Tarryall said, grinning, and motioned toward the street. "At least not this time. He's waiting for you in front of the hotel."

Blake understood then. Joe Klitz had sent Tarryall to look for him as soon as he heard that Blake was in town. Klitz was a gunman, a killer when his pride was hurt, and that pride had been mortally wounded by the licking Blake had given him.

Blake suspected that the ambush last night had not been Klitz's idea. That was more the style of Reeves and Tarryall. That had failed, and now Klitz was going to do it his way.

"I'll be there," Blake said.

Tarryall grinned wickedly. "He'll like that. Come smoking, mister."

Turning, Tarryall ran around the corner of the bank. Blake lifted his gun and examined it, then eased it back into the holster. He had started toward the street when the door of Thornton's office burst open and Hazel ran out.

"Just a minute, Carson," the girl said, catching his arm. "Are you sure you want to tackle Klitz?"

"Want me to run?"

"It might be better than getting yourself killed. After all, you won't be shooting at a quirt this time."

"Why the sudden interest in my well-being?" he asked.

"You're valuable to us alive," she answered candidly. "Dead, you're just another corpse."

"I figure on staying in this country for a while," he said. "I can't do that unless I settle this thing now."

"Then go right ahead," she snapped. "But remember, Joe Klitz is a lot handier with a gun than he is with his fists."

"I figured it that way," Blake said.

Hazel turned back toward the office. "Don't forget you're a tenderfoot, Mr. Carson," she said tauntingly.

Blake turned the corner of the bank and stopped. The street was empty. Tarryall had spread the word. Klitz stood on the porch of the hotel, leaning against a post as he smoked a brown-paper cigarette. When he saw Blake he tossed the stub into the dust, moved away from the post and hitched up his gun belt. Then he stepped importantly off the porch. It was, Blake thought, a grandstand act for the benefit of the townsmen who were peering out through windows and doorways along the street.

With slow steps Klitz moved toward Blake. Blake stepped out then, right hand swinging at his side, inches from his gun. Klitz was confident, but he was a treacherous man, the kind who would use any trick he could to gain an advantage. Twenty paces apart they stopped as if by mutual agreement.

"I figured you'd run," Klitz said.

"Not this morning. You don't look any bigger than you did."

"We're fighting my way this time," Klitz said with cool confidence. "No man licks me and lives to brag about it."

Klitz had said his piece. Blake saw that; he caught the sudden burst of light in the man's eyes, the down-drop of his right shoulder as Klitz made his draw. Blake's hand started downward in the same instant.

Gun thunder rocked the street, the echoes racing out across the prairie. Blake stood motionless, smoking gun held at his side, and watched amazement spread over Klitz's face, for it had been Blake's gun that had spoken the first and deciding word. Then Klitz broke at hip and knee and spilled forward, dust stirring around him.

Blake turned away, sick. This was not what he had come back for; it was not what he wanted. Men poured into the street, but Blake did not wait. He crossed to his horse and mounted. As he started to rein away, the sheriff moved out of the crowd toward him.

"I saw it, Carson," Ainsley said. "It was a fair fight. I won't arrest you."

"Thanks," Blake said with biting sarcasm. "That's mighty generous."

Ainsley frowned, started to say something, then pivoted on his heel and strode away. Blake pulled his horse around but stopped again when he saw Hazel Thornton come around the corner of the bank. She walked quickly to him and stopped by his horse, one hand running along the bay's neck.

"You're mighty fast for a tenderfoot, Mr. Carson," the girl said.

"Any law against it?" he asked.

"Maybe. You see, Adam York never hinted that his nephew was a gunslinger."

"Maybe York doesn't tell all he knows."

"Or maybe he doesn't know everything." She stepped closer to him and lowered her voice. "The offer we made still goes — Dan Blake."

She turned toward the bank and walked away as Blake reined into the street.

He would have ridden out of town if he hadn't glanced back at the men gathered in the street. Adam York was striding away from the others. He stepped up on the porch of the hotel.

Wheeling his horse, Blake trotted him back to the front of the hotel and dismounted. He wondered if anyone else had reached the same conclusion that Hazel Thornton had. It was a chance he would have to take. Running wouldn't do any good now. Looping the reins around the hitchrack, he ducked under the rail and stepped up on the porch where York was waiting.

"Where's the crew?" Blake asked.

Scowling, York lowered his head. "I can't understand it, Clyde. I've been in this country longer than any man I know. Until the last few weeks I've been able to hire or fire men whenever I wanted to. I just don't savvy."

Blake saw the bewilderment in the old man's eyes. Mostly it was wounded pride, but self-pity and anger were there, too.

"You mean you can't hire a crew?"

"That's what it amounts to," York said. "There were ten men without jobs in town today, but they all say they don't want to work. It isn't right, Clyde."

Blake shot a glance at the bank, thinking of the fat man sitting in there twiddling his pudgy fingers and of the little office behind the bank where George Thornton held sway. He felt pretty sure one or both of them was responsible, but he didn't say as much to York.

"I reckon I can hold down the Lazy B alone," he said, "but I won't get much work done."

A smile of sorts twisted York's mustache. "I'm not worried about you not being able to take care of yourself after what I just saw. I'm about ready to believe in miracles."

"That was no miracle," Blake said. "Klitz just wasn't as fast as he thought he was."

Blake stepped down from the porch and ducked back under the hitchrack. York followed him.

"I'll get some men and send them out as soon as I can," he said. "You'd better watch your step, Clyde. Klitz had a few friends."

Blake flipped the reins loose from the bar and mounted. "I'll keep my eyes open. And don't worry about getting a crew out there. I'll make out."

He whirled his horse, churning up a sheet of dust that the wind whipped off to the southeast as he rode out of town.

CHAPTER
TWELVE

From the window of Cruller's General Store, Kerry York watched the dust stirred up by the departing rider drift away on the strong breeze.

She saw her father come off the hotel porch and head for the back of Cruller's store. Evidently he was coming over to see if Sid Taylor was getting his load of salt on the wagon.

She turned back into the store, the biggest problem facing her crowding everything else out of her mind. In a few days she would be Mrs. Sid Saylor. She wanted more time to get ready for the wedding. But Sid and her father had suddenly decided that time had run out. She was in town this morning because Adam had told her to come in and pick out the things she needed.

She went through the back door to where Sid was loading sacks of salt from the platform into the wagon. Adam York came around the corner of the store just then.

"Got it all loaded, Sid?"

"About," Sid said, grunting as he heaved another sack of salt across onto the wagon.

"Got your trading done, Kerry?" Adam asked.

"Not yet," Kerry said. "I want to look around awhile."

"You haven't got long," Adam said. "The wedding's tomorrow."

Kerry caught her breath. "Tomorrow?" she gasped. "That's impossible."

"I don't see why. Do you, Sid?"

Sid grinned and shook his head. "I don't see why at all."

"But I'm not ready."

"We've been talking about it for a year," Sid said. "Why aren't you ready?"

"I've got to make my wedding dress and a hundred things. I don't even have the cloth bought yet."

"Well, get to buying, girl," Adam said impatiently.

"I can't possibly make the dress in less than three days," Kerry objected.

"Then you'll have to wear one of the dresses you've got. What difference does the dress make, anyway? It's you Sid is marrying, not your clothes."

"But I can't be ready," Kerry said stubbornly.

She knew her arguments were going to get her nowhere. She never had been able to go against Adam York's will and win.

"There's no time for arguing, Kerry," Adam said, his voice gentler than usual. He stepped up on the platform close to her. "I'm getting old. No sense in trying to hide it. Somebody younger is going to have to fill my shoes, Kerry. That man has to be your husband. He's got to be a man big enough and strong enough to hold what

I've clawed out of this prairie in my lifetime. Sid's that man. The wedding is tomorrow."

He stepped off the platform into the wagon with Sid, who had finished loading the salt and had climbed into the seat.

"Get your trading done fast, Kerry, and come on home," Adam said. "If you've got any sewing or fancy doodads to get ready, it will have to be today."

"You don't need anything fancy," Sid said as he clucked to the team. "You're pretty enough as you are."

Kerry watched the wagon pull out of the alley and turn down the street that led out toward the Flying Y. She couldn't be angry at her father. After all, he was doing what he thought best and doing it the only way he knew how, simply by declaring that it would be done. Opposition was something he could neither understand nor tolerate.

She turned back into the store. She'd have to make her purchases quickly. There was an awful lot to do.

She went to the dry goods counter and moved slowly from one bolt to another. She was going to have a wedding dress such as she wanted. She might not have it ready to wear for her wedding, but she would have it some day.

She heard the door open and saw Ben Evans come in. She turned quickly back to the cloth and concentrated on its texture. Once she had considered Ben Evans a firm friend of the family. But since her visit to his office yesterday, she couldn't think of Ben Evans without a crawling sensation.

He knew she was in the store. Kerry could feel his eyes on the back of her neck. But she didn't turn around. And after a minute, he went outside. She wondered if he had come in to buy something or if he had come in to talk to her. If the latter, he might be waiting to catch her when she left the store.

She decided on the cloth and how many yards she would need. The clerk was measuring the cloth off the bolt when Hazel Thornton came into the store. She came along the counter and stopped at Kerry's elbow.

"Pretty cloth," she said admiringly. "New dress?"

Kerry nodded. She didn't particularly like Hazel Thornton, although she couldn't put a finger on the reason. There was something about George and Hazel Thornton that posed a threat to the Flying Y.

"Fixing yourself up pretty for that cousin of yours?" Hazel asked.

Kerry felt herself blushing in spite of herself.

"It's not for Clyde," she said.

"That cousin of yours is quite a gunhand," Hazel said.

"I didn't know he was so good," Kerry admitted.

Hazel laughed shortly. "Neither did Klitz. What does your old man think of his nephew killing off his best hands?"

Kerry looked at Hazel quickly. Evidently she had heard about the ambush last night when Clyde had killed Bud Reeves.

"Pa doesn't blame Clyde," she said.

"Does your pa put a lot of trust in Carson?"

"Of course," Kerry said, wondering what Hazel was working up to.

"Maybe he ought to listen to him a little more. That cousin of yours has good sense about some things: mainly, the best thing for your old man to do."

"How do you know what Clyde thinks?" Kerry asked sharply.

Hazel smiled wisely and turned away. "I know a lot of things you would never suspect, dearie."

Kerry watched her go out of the store, wondering why she had come in.

It took Kerry another fifteen minutes to finish her shopping. When it was done and she had all her bundles under her arms, she hurried out of the store to her buggy, tossed in the bundles haphazardly and climbed in, clucking to the team almost before she was seated.

As she drove down the street, she shot a glance at the bank. Ben Evans was standing in the doorway as if he'd gotten that far on an errand and suddenly remembered he didn't need to finish it.

She knew she had guessed right. Evans had planned to intercept her at the buggy but she had moved too fast.

Kerry was two or three miles from town, driving her team hard, when she noticed a rider ahead of her. At first she gave the rider little thought. But when the rider kept right on into Flying Y range, her interest quickened. And it became even keener when she decided the rider was a woman.

The rider left the main trail and headed downstream on the south side of the creek. Kerry kept straight on until the first hill hid her from the rider; then she reined to the east, too. She drove cautiously, wishing she had her horse now instead of this buggy. The only woman she could think of who rode astride like a man was Hazel Thornton. If it was Hazel, Kerry wanted to know what she was doing on Flying Y range.

Kerry moved rapidly over the rolling hills and across the gullies that pointed into the hills from the creek like crooked fingers, but she saw no sign of the rider. Then she came to the top of a little hill from which she could see the old abandoned soddy on the slough.

She reined in quickly, for in front of the old soddy were two horses. One belonged to the rider Kerry had been following. The other was Sid Saylor's favorite mount.

She backed her team a little so the buggy couldn't be spotted from the soddy, then stood up so she could see over the top of the knoll. There was no doubt about it. That was Hazel talking to Sid.

Kerry stayed there for a few minutes, then turned the buggy around toward the Flying Y buildings. She couldn't learn anything from this far away, and there was no way to get closer without being seen. And what would Sid think if he caught her spying on him?

While she put her team away, she thought of the sewing she had to do. She couldn't get it done in time for tomorrow's wedding; she'd have to wear some dress she already had made. So perhaps she could ask Clyde for advice.

She took her bundles to the house. Adam York wasn't in sight, and all the men except Sid had gone out this morning on spring roundup on the south range, with Peter Swager in charge in Sid's place. Sid wasn't back yet from his rendezvous with Hazel Thornton. There was nobody to stop her from leaving.

It took only a few minutes to saddle her favorite pony. She rode east toward the Lazy B, going through the hills rather than along the creek so as not to meet Sid if he happened to be coming back from the soddy.

She hadn't thought about how jumpy Clyde was certain to be until after she had ridden boldly into the Lazy B yard and Clyde had suddenly burst out of the door, gun in hand.

"Don't shoot," she said with a laugh when she recovered from her surprise.

He holstered the gun sheepishly and came down the porch steps in one leap.

"I'm sorry, Kerry. I didn't know who might be riding in. Is anything wrong?"

She smiled, feeling a warm glow at his obvious concern. "Nothing that calls for you to break your neck coming to my rescue. I just — well, I had to talk to somebody."

"I'm a good listener," he said, a grin spreading over his face, changing it from the serious face of a desperate man to the handsome boyishness she liked so well. "Are you having trouble over on the Flying Y?"

"A little. But it's not shooting trouble. You seem to have a corner on all that. May I come in?"

"Of course." He moved quickly to help her dismount. "You sort of surprised me, riding in this way. I'm afraid you won't think much of my housekeeping. I haven't had much time to clean the place up after the other tenants left."

"I guess you have been busy." She walked ahead of him across the porch and into the big living room. "I saw what happened in town today. Where did you learn to handle a gun like that?"

He moved a chair around for her, and she dropped in it. "I've been west of the Mississippi before. Then I guess some things just come naturally to some people."

"You don't look like a natural gunman, Clyde. You were lucky today. But you're a marked man now."

He nodded slowly. "Maybe. But who is there to mark me except Tarryall? I don't think he'll buck me."

"He won't face you, not after what he saw in town today. There aren't many men around who would want to face you in a fair fight. But there are other ways."

He nodded. "Such as last night? That didn't work too well, either."

"Don't be too confident, Clyde," Kerry said.

"I won't overstep," he said, then hunched his chair closer to her. "You didn't ride over here just to give me a lecture."

"No," Kerry admitted. "I was thinking of my own troubles."

"Your pa?"

"In a way, but not about the note he owes Ben Evans as you're probably thinking."

She looked at him, wondering if she should tell him her personal troubles. After all, even though he was a cousin, he was almost a stranger. Her troubles meant nothing to him. But she had ridden all the way over there just to talk to him. She wouldn't back out now.

"I'm worried about myself, Clyde," she said. "I had to talk to somebody. This time I couldn't talk to Pa, so I came to you. You're the only other relative I have in the country."

She saw an odd look cross his face and wondered if he resented being dragged into problems that were none of his affair.

"Why couldn't you talk to your pa?" he asked.

She tried to smile. "I guess we're both too stubborn. We're on different sides of the fence on this. Maybe I'm just being temperamental. Pa says all women are. But I don't like to be pushed."

"Who's pushing?"

"Sid. And Pa's backing him. They want the wedding tomorrow."

"Tomorrow?" he exploded.

"That shouldn't shock you. You're not the one Sid wants to marry."

But she could see that it did shock him, and it gave her a warm glow. He was interested in her troubles, and he was on her side, too.

"Why tomorrow?" he asked.

"Sid's been pressing for an early wedding, and you remember he said he could get the money Pa needs to pay off Mr. Evans. Then something happened in town today that spurred Pa. I think it was the fact that he couldn't hire a crew for you. It finally made him see that he can't do everything the way he used to. He wants a younger man ready to take over the Flying Y when he has to quit, and Sid's that man. But Sid won't take the responsibility unless he's one of the family."

"I can understand that. But any man ought to know that a woman sets her wedding date. Your pa can't make you do it, Kerry."

He paced the floor, and Kerry detected the anger in his voice and in his steps.

"Pa isn't used to being stopped, Clyde, especially when he thinks he is right. And this time he honestly believes he is doing what is best for me and the ranch. Maybe he's right. I'm going to marry Sid some day. Maybe it doesn't make any difference when."

"Your pa has no business setting the date," he said, and now there was no doubt about the anger in his voice. "A man is born to live just one life. He's getting too big for his boots when he tries to run everybody else's."

Anger surged up in Kerry. "Don't talk like that about Pa. He's trying to do what's best for me."

"He's sure got a queer way of showing it." Then the anger drained out of his face. "I'm sorry, Kerry, but I just don't like the notion of you marrying Sid Saylor."

"What have you got against Sid?"

"Nothing. But you don't love him."

Anger poured through her again. "Of course I do," she said sharply. "Who says I don't?"

He faced her, standing very close, looking down at her. "You've just said it, Kerry," he said softly. "If you

105

loved him, tomorrow would be as good a wedding day as any. The whole trouble is that Adam York has run you like he has run everybody else. He says you're going to marry Sid, so you figure that's what you have to do. But now that the time has come, you want to put it off."

"Maybe you're right," she said, her voice little more than a whisper.

"I'm sure I'm right. Now you go home and tell your pa that you've changed your mind."

"I can't do that, Clyde," she said, feeling as miserable as she had ever felt in her life. "I just can't. It would break his heart. He's planned on this for years, and he's trained Sid to take over the Flying Y. He's never ever considered the possibility that Sid and I might not get married."

"Then it's about time he considered the fact that you've got your own life to live," he said hotly.

Kerry put a hand on his arm, her mind coming out of its daze at last. She knew now what she had to do.

"He's done a lot for me, Clyde," she said. "And he's still doing what he thinks is best. I won't let him down. You've straightened out my thinking, and I'm grateful, but I won't be foolish and let my silly romantic dreams get the best of me."

"But it isn't right!" he exploded.

"It is right. It will hold the Flying Y together, and that's what Pa wants. I guess nothing is more important than that."

For a moment she thought he was going to try to slap her into his way of thinking. Then his face softened, and there was a tenderness in his eyes she couldn't understand. He wheeled and made a tour of the room, his boot heels clicking sharply. When he stopped in front of her again, his face was rigid and expressionless.

"I reckon I've said enough," he said, tight-lipped.

He would have turned away again if she hadn't caught his arm. She could see that he was almost biting his tongue to keep from saying more. "There's something else you want to say, Clyde. What is it?"

The next instant she was sorry she had asked. He wheeled back to her, his face undergoing a dramatic change. There was the same fierce determination there now that she had seen when he faced Joe Klitz in the street of Winner.

He reached out and pulled her to him with such suddenness that she barely had time to catch her breath before he kissed her. Vaguely her conscience drummed at her that this wasn't right. Clyde was her cousin. He had no right to do this. And she had no right to cling to him this way. Yet she was doing it.

Then her conscience mastered her emotions and she pushed away from him. He released her and stepped back as though expecting to feel the blast of her anger. But she wasn't angry. She pushed her hair back in place.

"Why did you do that, Clyde?" she asked when she had gained control of her voice.

"I lost my head. I'm sorry."

She looked out across the yard to the river. "Don't blame yourself, Clyde. Since we are cousins, I took too much for granted. I guess we're more like strangers than cousins. I shouldn't have brought my troubles to you this way."

He started to say something, then checked himself. "What about your wedding?" he asked finally.

"It will go on as Pa planned it. I guess I don't love Sid as much as I should, but I'll marry him."

He frowned and turned to look out the window. "Do you want me to ride over and say my piece? Maybe I could convince your pa that the wedding ought to be postponed till you set the date."

She grasped at the straw. "Would you, Clyde? If he'd just put it off for a few days —"

He turned back, the reckless smile on his face again. "Sure. I probably won't have any luck, but I'll try."

CHAPTER
THIRTEEN

Darkness had swallowed the world when Blake and Kerry rode into the Flying Y yard. After caring for the horses, Blake learned from a couple of men who had ridden in from the round-up camp that both Saylor and York were out looking for Kerry. They'd be plenty peeved when they found out where she had been, but there was nothing he could do about it tonight. He had supper and, going to the bunkhouse, turned into the first empty bunk he came to.

Blake ate breakfast with the two Flying Y punchers before they headed back to the round-up camp, then went up to the house. The sooner he saw York, the better. There was no point in postponing the chore he had cut out for himself. He didn't expect to change York's mind, but he had to make the try before he could feel free to take the steps he had decided on during a sleepless night. One thing was certain. Kerry wanted a few more days' time before getting married, and she was going to get them. This day was not going to go as Saylor and York had planned.

When Blake knocked on the door, York boomed an invitation for him to come in. Saylor was in the house, too.

"Glad you're here, Clyde," York said contentedly. "Saves me the trouble of sending word over to you. This is a mighty special day. I couldn't let you miss your cousin's wedding."

"I wouldn't want to miss it."

York showed surprise. "Did Kerry tell you about it?"

Blake nodded. "Seemed pretty sudden. I gathered the date wasn't Kerry's idea."

"It wasn't exactly," York admitted, "but she knew it was coming. It just happened that today is the most convenient time for everyone."

"For Kerry, too? Did you ever think she might want to set the date?"

York frowned. "What in tarnation are you driving at, Clyde?"

"Why, I've always heard that girls get their biggest thrill out of making plans for their wedding. Strikes me you're cheating Kerry."

"Now see here, Clyde!" York reared up in his chair, eyes hot with a rush of anger. "Don't accuse me of cheating Kerry. I've given her the best of everything."

"Everything but the right to do something as she pleases."

"She's been planning this for a long time," York said defensively. "Just exactly when it happens doesn't make any difference."

"If it doesn't, give her a few more days. It means a lot to her."

"Just how do you know so much about what Kerry wants?" Saylor demanded.

Blake turned to face him. It was the first straight look he'd had at the man since he'd come into the room. Saylor was uncomfortable. For a fleeting second Blake wondered if there was more man in the Flying Y ramrod than he had given him credit for. Then he dismissed the idea. Anyone who would bargain as Saylor and York had and then force Kerry to submit to the plan was no part of a man.

"She told me a little, and I've got eyes even if you haven't. She doesn't want to marry you today, which you could see if you looked."

"You've opened your mug once too often, Clyde," York bellowed. "The plans are made and we're going ahead with them. Sid, you'd better start for the preacher."

"Well," Blake said sarcastically, "so you're going to have all the trimmings!"

"Kerry's request," Saylor said as he went through the door.

"She's getting everything she wants," York said, glaring at Blake. "There'll come a day when she'll be glad I did what I did."

It was like York, Blake thought. No one, not even his own daughter, could be right if she disagreed with him.

"There'll come a day when she'll finally see what you've done to her life and she'll hate you," Blake said evenly.

"Shut up!" the old man shouted. "If you weren't my nephew, I'd gun-whip you right where you stand."

"I wouldn't try if I were you," Blake said. "I reckon I'd better be riding."

"That's right," York agreed. "Get along before I forget you're Kerry's cousin. If you cause any trouble, so help me, I'll have your hide and you'll be out of a job."

"You can take my job, I reckon," Blake said, "but you'll have a sweet time getting my hide."

Blake wheeled toward the door. He had reasons of his own for wanting to be in the saddle. As he cut through the yard toward the corral, he saw Saylor splashing across the creek and urging his horse up the other bank. Blake lost no time in catching his horse and saddling him. In three minutes, he was crossing the stream on Saylor's trail.

The Flying Y ramrod was riding hard, but Blake didn't let him get out of sight. He had to overtake him before he reached Winner. What happened after he caught Saylor depended entirely upon the Flying Y foreman. One purpose prodded Blake — to see that Saylor did not take a preacher back to the Flying Y.

Blake was unable to catch Saylor until the town was in sight. When he came close enough to call to him, Saylor turned. Seeing who it was, he reined up and waited.

"You're in some hurry," Blake said, pulling in beside him.

For a moment Saylor didn't answer. He turned in his saddle to stare at the town that lay just ahead; then he said, "I've got a job to do." There was a tightness in his voice that Blake hadn't noticed back at the ranch.

"I've got some things to say to you before you get to town," Blake said.

Saylor nodded. "I expected something out of you. Seemed like you were taking Kerry's wedding kind of hard."

"I want her to get a square deal," Blake said. "You're not going after the preacher and you're not marrying Kerry today."

Saylor cocked an eyebrow. "You haven't yet said anything I wasn't expecting. Keep talking."

"What are you going to do?" Blake demanded.

"I'm going into town to do the job I came for."

"You're not taking a preacher back to the Flying Y," Blake said doggedly, his thumb hooked in his gun belt.

Saylor sighed as though weary of the talk. "Last night while York was out looking for Kerry, I went to town. I talked to a man about a deal we had. He backed out on me. I figure on making him keep his end of the bargain this morning."

Blake studied Saylor's face but learned nothing. "Then you're not going after a preacher?"

"The man I'm going to see is no sky pilot. He's on the other side of the fence."

Blake shifted uneasily in his saddle. He had expected trouble, either with fists or guns, when he confronted Saylor. But apparently there was to be none. He wasn't certain what to do. He couldn't drag Saylor off his horse and hog-tie him for no reason. And Saylor was being careful not to give him a reason. He'd have to wait and see if Saylor stood by his word not to bring a preacher back to the ranch.

Blake motioned toward town. "Slope along. But get one thing straight. Don't bring a preacher."

Saylor laughed dryly. "Why not? They use preachers for funerals as well as weddings, you know."

The foreman kicked his horse into a lope toward town, giving Blake his back. Blake followed slowly.

Dan rode along Main Street, tabulating everything in sight. His eyes riveted for a moment on Saylor's horse at the hitchrack in front of the bank. The reins were not fastened to the bar, but were dangling, holding the animal ground-hitched. Blake pulled up, wondering about this. A man would not leave his mount that way unless he planned a quick getaway.

Thoughtfully Blake reined his horse in beside Saylor's and dismounted. He dropped his reins as Saylor had done and stepped up on the boardwalk. If Saylor aimed to split the breeze getting out of town, Blake might find the same speed necessary.

Blake had started past the bank, intended to look in the saloon for Saylor, when a rattle of shots broke the morning quiet. Wheeling, Blake raced for the corner of the bank. Apparently the shots had come from the back of the building. That would be Thornton's office.

As Blake cleared the corner, he saw Saylor reel out of the little office, gun in one hand and a small sack in the other. A gun roared again. Saylor jerked and stumbled, his face contorted with pain. He regained his feet and came on toward the front of the bank.

Impulsively Blake ran toward him. Saylor saw him and staggered his way, holding out the sack. "Take it," the foreman breathed. "Give it to York."

"What is it?" Blake demanded as he took the sack.

A bullet from the office doorway snapped by Blake's head. "Take it," Saylor said thickly. "It's something I owe York. I'll never get it to him."

Blake shoved Saylor toward the horses in front of the bank. Whipping out his gun, he fired a shot that splintered the door casing an inch from the spot where a man's head was showing again to line the sights of a gun. The head disappeared.

Blake swung back and helped Saylor into the saddle. He vaulted into his own saddle and wheeled into the street. Thornton appeared in the doorway of his office and snapped a shot at them as they left town. Turning in his saddle, Blake sent the man scurrying back through the door with a well-placed shot. Then he bent low and urged his horse after Saylor's, which was two lengths ahead of him.

Pursuit would soon be organized, but each minute put Blake and Saylor farther ahead. As he rode close to the Flying Y foreman, Blake asked himself why he had taken a hand. Apparently Saylor had held up Thornton. Blake had been on halfway friendly terms with Thornton. Now, by helping Saylor escape, Blake had not only queered himself with Thornton but had also gotten himself into a jam with the law.

They were a mile out of town when Blake realized that Saylor wasn't going to stay in the saddle much longer. He was hard hit, although Blake could not tell just how badly. A soddy loomed ahead of them. They passed the house and then reined in behind the barn, Blake pulling Saylor's horse up beside his.

As Blake stopped out of sight of the trail, Saylor leaned weakly on his saddle horn and started to slide sideways. Blake hit the ground and reached the Flying Y ramrod before he fell. He eased him down and set him against the barn wall, looking quickly at his wounds. One was a hole through the flesh under his left arm; the other was high in his chest. That was the one which had done the damage. If Saylor could be taken to a doctor immediately, he might have a chance. The exertion of the flight from town hadn't helped his condition any.

Blake stepped to the corner of the barn. The house looked empty but the place wasn't abandoned. Apparently the people who lived there were not home right at the moment.

Dan glanced down the road toward town. At any minute now a posse would come thundering down that road. All he and Saylor could do was hide. He didn't dare take Saylor back toward town now. Yet town and Dr. Gentry were Saylor's only chance.

"Coming yet?" Saylor asked when Blake turned back.

"They will be. I'll help you inside the barn. We'll hide the horses and hope."

By the time Blake had helped Saylor inside the barn and onto a bed of hay and gone back for the horses, he heard the pounding of hoofs. The posse was coming.

Hurriedly Blake led the two horses into the back door of the barn and closed the door. Then he hunched down beside Saylor and listened to the horses approaching outside.

"Why don't you light out?" Saylor said, his breath coming in little jerks as though he had just finished a long hard run. "This isn't your scrap."

"I've been thinking about it," Blake said. "But you need a doc."

"Nothing you can do about that. Take that money bag to York. That's all I ask."

"Want me to step out there now where the posse will see me?"

"Of course not." Saylor's face twisted with pain. "Maybe they'll go on by. If they do, you head for the Flying Y with the money."

"How much money is in that bag?" Blake said.

"Ten thousand. York needs that much to get Evans off his neck. I promised him I'd get it for him."

Blake nodded. "I heard you tell him. But I don't reckon he figured on you getting it this way."

Saylor grinned weakly. "There are a lot of things he didn't figure on."

The thunder of the posse drew even with the barn and faded away without a pause. Blake breathed more easily. If they should catch him with Saylor, he would be branded as guilty as the Flying Y foreman. Just why he had stayed with Saylor until now was something he couldn't quite understand himself.

"You seemed determined this morning to keep me from marrying Kerry," Saylor said as if reading Blake's thoughts. "Why don't you ride out, now that the posse is gone, and leave me here to die? Then Kerry won't be marrying me."

Blake studied the man's face, which was twitching with pain. "Maybe I should," he said. "But I never walked off and left a crippled critter on the range without doing what I could for him or putting him out of his misery."

Saylor glared at Blake. "You've got a gun. What are you waiting for?"

The look in his eyes told Blake that Saylor wasn't joking.

"I figure you've got a chance if I get you to Dr. Gentry," Blake said. "So I'm sticking with you. When do you think you can ride?"

Saylor didn't get a chance to answer. Outside the barn leather squeaked, followed by other muffled sounds Blake couldn't distinguish.

"Some of the posse must have come back," Saylor whispered. Blake saw that he wasn't quite as ready to die as he had seemed a minute before, for he fumbled for his gun, getting it in his hand and facing the front door.

Blake faced the door, too, faced it with a drawn gun.

CHAPTER
FOURTEEN

Blake half expected the man or men outside to charge through the door, guns blazing. But instead the door opened easily and a small, sad-faced farmer came through, leading a team of horses.

The farmer stopped short when he saw Blake and Saylor, his jaw dropping at sight of the guns.

"Who are you?" he asked finally.

Blake put up his gun. "We were just resting here in your barn."

"You're the ones who held up Thornton's office in town," the famer said. "But they said that only one man did that."

"There was only one," Saylor said. "This fellow is just trying to save my hide."

Excitement was replacing the pallor in the farmer's face. "You'll have to get out of here. I don't want to be mixed up in this. Get! Get!"

"Now keep your shirt on," Blake said. "We'll get out as soon as it's dark."

"Dark?" Hysteria was beginning to creep into the man's voice. "You'll get out now. If the sheriff finds you here, I'll be in trouble, too. Get!"

"The sheriff went past here ten minutes ago," Blake said. "He didn't look then. He won't look when he comes back."

"If you don't get out, I'll go tell the sheriff you're here!"

"That might not be healthy," Saylor said. Blake saw that he still held his gun.

The farmer saw it, too. "All right, all right," he said. "But don't let my wife find you here. She'll do something. She might start shooting."

Blake saw that the man was more afraid of his wife than he was of them. "Where was your wife when we came in here?" he asked.

"She was in town with me. The nose of my plow gave out and I had to take it to the blacksmith. My wife went along to do the trading."

Blake looked at Saylor. "Feel like riding?"

"If you can think of any place to ride to," Saylor said.

A sudden shrill call came from the house. "Jerome! What's wrong out there?"

"That's my wife," the man said excitedly. "You'd better run."

"How did she know anything was wrong out here?" Blake asked.

"I wish I knew how she figures out things like that," the man said. "But you'd better light a shuck out of here unless you want to face the old lady's shotgun."

Saylor struggled to a sitting position. "I'm carrying all the lead I can handle. I'm not hankering for a load of buckshot, too."

120

"She wouldn't shoot if we used you as our shield," Blake said.

"I wouldn't bet on that," the man said. "She's threatened to shoot me plenty of times. Don't give her an excuse to do it."

It would have been almost funny if it hadn't been so serious.

Blake helped Saylor into his saddle and steadied him there. "Think you can hang on?"

"Sure," Saylor said. "I feel better than I did. I can ride pretty good if somebody's going to put a load of buckshot in my tail. Let's go."

The farmer opened the back door of the barn and stood back to let Blake lead his horse and Saylor's outside. Then Blake mounted and led the way west at right angles to the road that ran south in front of the barn.

He glanced back once and saw the man talking to his wife. She was standing at the door of the soddy and, sure enough, she had a shotgun in her hands.

Blake tried to settle on a course of action.

"We're going to circle back toward town," he finally decided.

"Want to get caught?" Saylor asked.

"We'll be safer there than out here."

Saylor made no more objections, and Blake reined around to the north. He rode slowly, partly on Saylor's account and partly to keep from attracting attention.

Blake aimed for the young grove of trees that had been planted just west of town by some ambitious homesteader who had taken the land right next to the town plot. The trees weren't very big, but they were big enough to cut off the view of the town from anything southwest, and they would hide a horse and rider once they were in the grove.

Blake saw no movement, and they weren't challenged as they rode into the grove. Blake thought of holing up here till dark. But he realized that, in spite of the sparse shade afforded by the trees, it would be too hot for Saylor. He had to have a roof over his head.

From the eastern edge of the grove, Blake studied the town. One of the closest buildings was a barn half a block west of Ben Evans' big house. It was probably Evans' barn, but this was no time to be choosy. Anyway, it might be the safest place. Ben Evans wouldn't be riding anywhere during the heat of the day, so that barn would probably not be touched all day.

"We'll go over to that barn," Blake decided.

Saylor didn't say anything. He was slumped over his saddle, using what strength he had left to keep himself on the horse.

Blake led the way out of the trees to the barn, almost holding his breath. People were bound to be stirring about somewhere in town. If they happened to look this way they'd know at a glance what the situation was. There was no disguising a wounded man slumped over a saddle.

But there was no challenge before they reached the barn. All Blake could do was hope no one had seen them. Inside the barn, Blake got Saylor off the horse and made him as comfortable as he could. Then he loosened the cinches on the horses but left them saddled. They might have to leave in a hurry.

"I'll slip over to the doc's office now," Blake said.

"It won't do any good," Saylor said, and Blake noticed the weakness of his voice. The ride in from that farm had been almost too much.

"The doc can fix you up."

"I doubt it," Saylor said. "Sit down. I've got something to tell you."

Blake squatted down beside Saylor. Noon had passed and the afternoon sun was halfway down the sky. It was hot and smelly in the barn, but better than it had been outside.

Dan looked at Saylor closely. The sweat on his forehead, the pallor of his face and the sagging of his lips told him what Saylor apparently already knew. Time was running out for the Flying Y foreman.

"What do you want to tell me?" Blake asked.

"Get that money to York," Saylor said, his words slurred together as though his tongue were too thick to work right. "It's for Kerry's sake. Promise?"

"Sure." Blake was silent for a minute. What was there to say to a dying man? Saylor was no friend of Blake's. Still, it wasn't easy to hunker beside him and watch him die.

"I wouldn't care about York if it wasn't for Kerry," Saylor said. "He's an old fool. He never suspected I was selling him out."

A shock ran over Blake. "Who'd you sell out to?" he demanded.

"Thornton. He's supposed to be in cahoots with Evans. When Evans closed out York, Thornton was to start setting up his irrigation lay-out." Saylor paused to get his breath and new strength. "Thornton's a bigger crook than Evans. He was double-crossing Evans."

Blake knew Saylor was talking his life away but he wanted to talk and Blake wanted to hear.

"How could Thornton double-cross Evans?" he asked. "Evans will own the land when he forecloses."

"Thornton had a plan," Saylor said. "I was to marry Kerry. Thornton was going to give me ten thousand to give to York to pay off Evans. That would leave Evans holding the bag."

"How would Thornton come out on that?"

"Thornton was aiming to drygulch York. Then the Flying Y and the Lazy B would go to Kerry and me. I was to see that Thornton got it all."

Blake saw the picture then. As irrigated farms along the creek, the flat land of the Flying Y and the Lazy B were worth five times what York owed Evans. But by paying off Evans, Thornton would have it all to himself. Blake didn't any longer need to be told where Thornton had gotten the ten thousand dollars to give to York. No wonder Hazel had guessed he was Dan Blake. She had reason to know Clyde Carson was dead.

"Why did you have to steal the money from Thornton this morning?" Blake asked, determined to get the whole story as long as Saylor was disposed to talk.

"I went after the money last night," Saylor said, his words getting harder to understand all the time. "Thornton had new ideas. He had found a way to

124

blackmail Evans. He was going to buy the note from Evans for less than ten thousand. Then he could foreclose on York and not have to share anything with me. He'd double-cross his own mother."

"If you were willing to sell out York, why did you come back this morning to rob Thornton just to give the money to York?" It was the only phase of this thing that Blake didn't understand.

"Thornton and Evans are both skunks. No matter which one got York's land, it would have hurt Kerry. I love her, Blake. When the chips were down, I couldn't let anything happen to hurt her." Saylor tried to grin, but all he could manage was a twisted, slack-lipped grimace. "So I get myself drilled through the brisket. I'm a real tough badman, ain't I?"

Saylor slumped back on the hay, completely spent. Blake bent over him and heard his faint breathing. He was unconscious but still alive. Blake had risked his neck today to try to save Saylor's life. If he didn't want to lose the battle now, he had to get to the doctor soon.

He started for the door, then remembered the ten thousand dollars in his saddle bag. Going to his horse, he took out the money and buried it in one corner of the feed bin. If anybody should stumble onto Saylor's hiding place while Blake was gone, the first thing he would look for would be the money. Blake was determined to get that to York if possible.

That money would pay off Evans. It wouldn't end the trouble for York, but it would give him a reprieve. Without it, York would be broken and crushed. That was what Blake had come to this country to see. But now the anticipation had lost its savor. Blake faced the truth squarely. Shielding Kerry from harm was more important to him than collecting his revenge on Adam York.

Making certain no one was in sight, Blake left the barn and walked carelessly down the alley to the back of the doctor's office. The door was unlocked and he stepped inside, fighting down the urge to hurry. Anyone rushing around in this heat would attract attention quicker than a troop of cavalry parading down Main Street.

Dr. Gentry was in his office, slumped in his chair, staring at his boots.

"Busy, Doc?" Blake asked.

"I'm never busy," Gentry grumbled. "I wish that gunman had plugged Thornton this morning. I'd like to work on him."

There was no mistaking the malice in the doctor's voice, but Blake ignored it. He explained about Saylor, and the doctor stirred immediately.

"So he's the fellow who robbed Thornton?" Gentry said. "More power to him. I'll save him if I can. Where is he?"

"In a barn out back. We'd better hurry."

The doctor picked up his little bag and followed Blake across the alley and down to the barn. Saylor was still unconscious, and the doctor dropped on his knees beside him.

After a brief examination, he looked up at Blake. "We've got to get him to my office. That bullet has to come out."

"Think he'll make it?"

Gentry shook his head. "He'll be dead in an hour. But I've got to try. His only chance is to have that bullet taken out. Help me carry him."

Blake didn't like the idea of carrying Saylor across the alley. If anyone saw them, the law would be in the doctor's office in a matter of minutes, providing there was any law left in town.

But there was no alternative. Blake picked Saylor up by the shoulders while Gentry lifted his feet. They made their way across to the doctor's office, and Blake heard nothing to indicate they had been seen.

Blake stayed in the doctor's office while Gentry worked on Saylor. It was just sundown when Gentry came over to Blake, weariness lining his face.

"I tried," he said. "He never regained consciousness."

Blake stood up. "Thanks, Doc. I've got an errand to attend to. I'd better be at it."

"Wish that was Thornton there," Gentry said, staring at Saylor's body.

Blake wondered at the venom in the doctor's voice. Then he turned and went out the back door. Twilight had settled over the town, and there was much more stirring around now than there had been during the heat of the day.

Blake hesitated, wondering if he should stay in the shadow of the doctor's office until it was darker before risking detection by crossing the alley to the barn. He moved to the corner of the building and took a look into the street.

The posse was back, the men dismounting in front of the sheriff's office.

Blake might have waited in the shadows until complete darkness had enveloped the town if he hadn't seen Ben Evans come out of the barn, look around for a moment, then duck back inside. Evans must know now that Blake and Saylor were in town. He couldn't help seeing their horses in his barn. What was in the fat man's mind? Would he rush to tell Sheriff Ainsley? Or would he look for the money he knew Saylor had stolen from Thornton?

Blake guessed he'd look for the money. A greedy scheming mind like Evans' would find some way to take the money and never let anyone know he had it. Blake's only chance was to get to Evans before the banker found the money, hid it, then ran to Ainsley with his story.

Dropping into a crouch, Blake ran across the alley and down to the barn, feeling sure he had not been detected. He pressed himself against the wall close to the door and listened. He heard grunts and heavy breathing as Evans moved around inside. But he couldn't guess just what the banker was doing.

Then there came a loud sigh of obvious satisfaction. To Blake, that could mean only one thing. Evans had found what he was looking for.

Blake ducked into the barn, his eyes straining to see through the darkness. He made straight for the feed bin. For if Evans had found the money, he would still be there.

Blake heard Evans grunt like a surprised bear. Then he saw the banker claw at something under his coat and guessed it was the shoulder gun he had heard Evans was so handy at using.

Blake launched himself in a long dive and smashed into the fat man before he could get his gun free of its holster. Blake had a gun but he didn't want to use it there. He'd have the whole town on him in a matter of seconds and, even if he got away, it would only be to lead the posse in another chase. And this time he might not be lucky enough to elude capture.

Even as he fell, Evans kept trying to get his gun free. Blake concentrated on that pudgy hand clawing under the coat. The banker was flat on his back now, and Blake threw his weight against him, pining the hand against the banker's chest. Then he ripped the coat back and got the gun himself, tossing it into the darkness of a corner of the barn.

Evans kicked and struck out with his free hand, clawing like a cornered wildcat. He was surprisingly strong, but Blake had the advantage and he kept it.

"I'll get you for this, Blake," Evans panted.

Blake didn't even answer. He knew if he intended to get out of town without having the sheriff on his trail, he had to keep Evans out of reach of Ainsley for a while.

Evans kept pounding Blake in the ribs, as high as he could reach from his supine position. Blake brought his fist over Evans' arm and smashed it into the banker's jaw. Evans grunted and dropped his hand. Blake clipped him again, then got up. Ben Evans was out cold.

Blake searched Evans, but all his pockets were empty. Then his hand struck the money bag where Evans had dropped it at the corner of the feed bin. Blake stuffed it into his saddle bag.

Quickly Blake tightened the cinch on his saddle and let both his and Saylor's horses out the back door of the barn. Mounting his horse and leading Saylor's, he walked them slowly west into the grove of trees.

Once through the trees, he put the horses to a gallop toward the Flying Y.

CHAPTER
FIFTEEN

Darkness gripped the land as Blake came close to the Flying Y headquarters. He reined in a hundred yards from the building and waited, listening.

He heard nothing, and all he could see was one light in the big house. There was no light in the bunkhouse. But Blake knew the crew was out on roundup.

Blake ground-reined his horse fifty yards from the corral and went ahead on foot. After examining the corrals and the barn, he went back and got his horse. If Ainsley had left a man, he must be at the house.

After unsaddling his horse and feeding him, Blake took the money bag and headed for the house where the light still shone. He checked through a window before going inside. Only York and Kerry were in sight.

Kerry ran to the door when she heard him come in. "We've been so worried, Clyde," she said, putting a hand on his arm.

"Where's Sid?" York bawled as soon as he saw who it was.

Blake didn't answer, his eyes sweeping the rooms. "Had any visitors?"

Kerry nodded. "Sheriff Ainsley and a posse were here this morning. They came back a while before sundown."

"Thornton in it?"

Kerry nodded again. "He did most of the talking."

"Any of the outfit stay?"

"They all left. At least I think they did."

York crossed the room and thrust his nose into Blake's face. "I'm not asking you again. Where's Sid?"

Blake crossed the room and tossed the money bag on the table. "I'll tell you now that I know there isn't a lawman breathing down my neck."

"The sheriff wasn't after you, was he?" Kerry demanded.

"I didn't figure it was wise to let him find me just to prove it. Saylor and I weren't far ahead of the posse when we left town this morning."

"Thornton said Sid was hard hit," York said, trying to hide the quaver in his voice.

Blake nodded. "He's dead. He told me to give this sack to you."

"What's in it?" York asked, nodding at the bag.

"Saylor said there was ten thousand dollars."

York swore softly and leaped toward the table. "Where did he get it?"

"In Thornton's office. That's what kicked up the rumpus. Thornton didn't like the way Saylor took it."

"Then Thornton was telling the truth," Kerry breathed, her face showing the shock the news of Saylor's death had brought. "He said Sid held him up."

"This will pay Evans off," York exclaimed, the old fire coming back into his eyes.

"That's what Saylor intended for you to do," Blake said.

132

"How did you happen to be with Sid?" York asked.

"I'm not right sure myself. I was close to him when he came out of Thornton's office, and I took a hand. Just seemed the thing to do. He was in bad shape, but I helped him get out of town. We hid in a barn and let the posse go by. This afternoon I got him back to town to the doc. But the doc couldn't save him. He died about sundown."

"Sid was trying to help Pa," Kerry said softly. "He just took the wrong way to do it."

"He loved you," Blake said. "I didn't think he did, but I was wrong."

Kerry turned away, hiding the emotion that Blake knew must be showing in her face.

York picked up the money bag, staring at it while triumph built up his old arrogance.

"I'll show that nickel-nursing Ben Evans!" he chortled. "Sid's done his part. Now it's up to us. We'll take this money and throw it in Evans' face first thing in the morning."

"I think I'll stay close to the ranch," Blake said. "I doubt if I'd be appreciated around town until somebody cools off Ainsley."

"They never mentioned you today," York said. "They were looking for Sid, not you."

"They saw me help Sid get away," Blake said. "That will be enough to make Ainsley ask questions."

"I'll button his lip if he pipes up," York said. "I want you there to see Evans' face when I show him this money. I wonder if this could be the same money that was stolen from you." York rubbed his chin thoughtfully. "Not many people would have this much cash lying around."

"You will go with us, won't you?" Kerry asked.

"All right; I will," he agreed reluctantly . . .

Winner was quiet and peaceful when they rode into Main Street the next morning.

They dismounted in front of the bank and racked their horses. York led the way inside, Blake and Kerry following. He didn't stop at the window but marched straight on into Evans' office as he had done the other time Blake had been with him. But today there was one difference. George and Hazel Thornton were with Ben Evans.

"Well," Evans said testily, "forgot to knock as usual."

"Doors were made to open, not hammer to pieces," York snapped.

"What's on your mind?" Evans asked uneasily.

"This!" York tossed the sack of money on the desk. "Dig up my note. There's enough right here to pay what I owe."

Thornton let out a squawk. "That's my money. Saylor stole it."

"Prove it," York snapped. "You came tearing out to my ranch yesterday morning with a wild yarn about Saylor robbing you. Well, I haven't seen Sid since early yesterday morning. He didn't give me that money."

"Saylor's dead," Thornton said. "But we didn't find the money he stole. That's it right there."

"Prove it or shut up," York yelped. He wheeled on Evans. "Now let's have my note, Ben."

134

"Wait a minute." Thornton pointed to Blake. "He was with Saylor. He took a shot at me. He's the one who gave York the money."

"Let's see you prove that," York shot back. "Clyde's my right-hand man, and I don't hire lawbreakers."

Evans looked up from the money he had been counting, a cunning light playing across his flabby features.

"So he's your right-hand man, is he?" he said softly. "Maybe you'd like to know just who your right-hand man is, Adam."

York pounded a fist on Evans' desk. "I know who he is," he bellowed. "He's my nephew. He was bringing me the money to pay you off when he got robbed. I don't know how he got the money back and I don't care. All I know is I've got it. Cancel my note now, blast your hide!"

"Sure," Evans agreed softly. "But it's downright funny, having a Blake save your skin."

"Blake!" York roared. "He's Clyde Carson, you lying keg of lard! Don't call him a Blake!"

York started around the desk after Evans. The banker backed away, howling. "He's Dan Blake, I tell you."

York stopped, motioned to Blake. "Tell him he's the biggest liar in Nebraska, Clyde. Then I'm going to beat the tar out of him."

There was a moment of silence while every eye in the room turned on Blake.

"He's right, York," Blake said, wondering how York would react. "I'm Dan Blake, the son of the man you hired Ed Harms to kill."

"I didn't hire Ed to kill Jim Blake," York shouted. Then he seemed to grasp the meaning of Blake's admission and dug for his gun.

Blake had half expected that. Adam York's temper was like a keg of gunpowder with a short fuse. The name of Blake was just the match to light that fuse. At York's move, Blake's hand swept down with the same swiftness that had surprised Ed Harms and Joe Klitz. York's gun never cleared leather. He was staring into the muzzle of Blake's Colt, his hand wrapped around the butt of his gun.

"Don't try it, York," Blake said. "That goes for the rest of you. You stole the Lazy B, York, and now you own the land just for paying the back taxes. I reckon I won't get it back, but you won't keep it, either. Evans and Thornton aim to clean you out. Evans sent for me to kill Harms, which I did. But it was a fair fight, and the law doesn't have any charge against me."

"He's lying, York," Evans shouted. "So help me, he's lying as fast as his tongue can wag."

"I reckon," York muttered. "Me and Jim Blake never got along. If Harms hadn't plugged Jim, he'd have gotten me. It was building up to that." He shook his head. "But I don't know about you, Ben. This whole thing stinks to high heaven."

"Saylor got that ten thousand from Thornton's office," Blake said sharply. "Where do you suppose Thornton got it?"

"Why, I . . ." York chewed on his lower lip. He glowered at Thornton. "Somebody robbed Clyde."

136

"Exactly," Blake said. "The Thorntons knew I wasn't Carson. They knew that because they killed Carson. You told Evans about Carson bringing the money. Evans and Thornton are in this together; they aim to get your range so they can put in an irrigation project."

Thornton was on his feet now. He said evenly, "You know he's lying, York. It's my guess that Blake killed Carson and took his money and his horse and changed clothes with him."

"Yeah," York said heavily. "I could believe that as well as Blake's story."

Blake watched the men, glowering at him and hating him, but not daring to move. Then he looked at Kerry, who stood a couple of steps from her father. He saw shock on her face, but there was wistfulness there, too, as if she wanted to believe that this was a bad dream that she could forget. He brought his gaze back to York's craggy face.

"I've spent ten years hating you, York," Blake said slowly. "I figured you hired Harms to kill Dad, and I came back because Evans sent for me and said it was time to square things. I killed Harms, and I'm not sorry about that. Maybe I was wrong about you, maybe not, but I have found out some things I didn't know. You're just a jumpy old man about to lose his shirt to some slick crooks. You aren't riding high and handsome any more, and I'm kind of sorry, because I've found out I love Kerry. That's the reason I've been stringing along with you."

Blake backed out of Evans' office and ran to the front of the bank. The teller stared at him but made no move to interfere. Voices came from the office. None of them, not even York, cared to crowd his luck too far against the man who had gunned down Ed Harms and Joe Klitz.

Outside, Blake flipped the reins of his bay free of the hitchrail and vaulted into the saddle. As his horse hit the street in a run, he heard Thornton yell from the bank for the sheriff, but Thornton didn't use his gun.

Blake had the head start he needed. He let the bay out for the first two miles. There was no pursuit yet, but there would be soon. He grinned wryly, wondering if Ainsley was tired of riding. Well, it didn't make much difference about the sheriff. There was slim chance of the law catching him if his luck held.

He splashed across the creek and headed into the sand hills to the south. There he wound through the network of valleys and swales, aiming at a bald, wind-swept knoll that towered above its neighbors. He reached the top and, looking back, saw that the posse was on his trail. They would be convinced that he had not headed back to the Lazy B.

Once off the knoll, Blake swung toward the lower ranch. Tracking him over the thick carpet of grass that covered the bottoms of these valleys would be tedious work at best. He would, he thought, have time enough to get to the ranch and collect his stuff and be gone before he was located.

He pulled up in the edge of the hills flanking the Lazy B buildings. He waited there for a long moment, motionless, but there was no sign of life about the place. He rode down toward the house, then stopped, one hand falling to his gun, his eyes on the ground. There were fresh tracks in the yard. One horse, he decided. But one was enough. Someone had guessed he would come there.

Dismounting quickly, he ducked out of line with the windows and front door and moved quickly to the side of the building. There was no window between him and the door, and he slid along the wall until he was pressed against the door jamb. If someone was waiting inside, he was in for a surprise. Gun palmed, he jerked open the door and lunged in. He stopped, flat-footed, his gun muzzle sinking toward the floor. Hazel Thornton was sitting motionless in a chair, smiling at him.

"Lady," he breathed, "you just had one hand on the pearly gate."

The girl rose. "I came a little closer than I expected. I thought a horse might scare you off, so I hid mine. You must have a sixth sense."

"It comes in handy. How did you know I'd come here?"

"I just knew you would. I want to see you as bad as the posse does, only I'm smarter than Ainsley. He's trying to run you down in the hills; I came here and waited for you to come to me."

"Say your piece," Blake said. "I'm not staying here long."

"You lost the hounds in the hills, Dan. Sit down and listen. I've got a proposition to make."

"I heard your proposition before."

"Part of it, yes. And it didn't sound so bad, did it? Now there's more to it, and the situation is different, too. Before, you were in good with York. You know now where you stand with him. You've got plenty of reason to hate York. And you want part of the Lazy B for a cattle ranch of your own. Now I've got a proposition that will hand everything to you on a silver platter."

He stood motionless, looking at her and thinking that people like the Thorntons were always convinced that a man could be bought if the offer was good enough.

She came to stand close to him. "If you're hesitating because you think you're in love with that little fluff of a York girl," she said, her head flung back, her lips smiling, "you can just get her out of your head. She's not your kind, Dan." Her hands came to rest lightly on her arms; her smile was inviting. "I can make any man forget Kerry York if he's willing to let me try."

"You didn't make Sid Saylor forget Kerry."

She shook her head. "I didn't try. Sid was just a man who happened to be handy. I'm a good judge of men, Blake. Dad isn't. Saylor was Dad's idea. You're mine."

"Thanks," he said dryly. "Now just what is this proposition? The same one you offered Saylor?"

"How much did he tell you?"

"He told me quite a bit. For one thing, he said you aimed to double-cross Evans."

She studied his face for a minute before speaking. "Now you're getting down to the meat of things. Ben Evans took us in with him because he needed us. But he never intended for us to get anything out of it."

"Funny," Blake said. "That's the way Saylor had it figured, except he thought Evans was the one who was being used and who would come out on the short end of the stick."

"That's only because we were beating Evans to the punch. Haven't you wondered why Evans called you in when he did to gun down Harms?"

Blake thought for a moment.

"I reckon I have," he said finally.

"He had his reasons, and they weren't to help you get the Lazy B, either. Dad and I had Harms and Klitz working for us. Maybe you don't know it, but Ben Evans is very handy with that shoulder gun of his. Dad is not fast with a gun. We needed someone on our side who would make sure Evans didn't try some high-handed deal. Harms and Klitz were insurance against that. Evans knew that if he tried anything on us, either Harms or Klitz would get him. So he brought you in to get rid of Harms, thinking Klitz would high-tail it out of the country and that would put us right where he wanted us."

Blake could see now why Evans had wanted to hire him again after he had killed Harms — it had been to kill Klitz. And he understood why Hazel had been so concerned when he had been challenged to a gun fight by Klitz. She wanted Klitz to stay alive as a threat to Evans.

"So now you want me to be your protection," Blake said slowly.

Hazel nodded. "If Evans knew you were working for us, he'd be mighty careful not to try anything."

"Looks to me like Evans is out of it now that York has paid him off."

"Do you think Evans will give up that easy?"

"I have a hunch Evans likes to hide behind the law. And I don't see how he can do anything legally. For that matter, it looks to me like you're holding the sack, too, now that Saylor is dead and can't marry Kerry. Or maybe you figure on me taking Saylor's place."

Hazel laughed easily, her eyes bright with anticipation. "That's not what I had in mind for you. It's like I said, Dan. Kerry isn't your kind of woman."

"And you are? Is that it?"

"Do you doubt it? You underestimate me, Dan."

"Maybe."

He turned to look out the window.

"Listen to me, Dan," Hazel said, trying to pull his attention back to her. "We've tried the easy ways to get rid of York, and they failed. Now it's the hard way. You throw in with us and you'll get all the sand hill range of both the Flying Y and the Lazy B. Isn't that fair enough?"

"York holds the cards, now that he's paid off Evans."

"He doesn't own Ainsley. Ainsley will string along with whoever holds the whip hand. We're going to make sure he sees we hold that hand."

"And if I agree, you come with the deal?"

She laughed. "Not so fast. The man who gets me has to work for me."

He studied her face for a moment. It seemed soft and feminine; the inviting little smile still tugged at the corners of her mouth. But he wasn't fooled. She'd use him just as she had tried to use Sid Saylor, and when the time came, she'd double-cross him just as she

142

planned to do to Ben Evans. Well, that was a game two could play. If he intended to stay on, he'd better get his bets down and get into the game on one side or the other.

"What's the play?" he asked.

She walked away from him, looking out the window in turn. "I said we had to do it the hard way. Evans will stick with us. He doesn't know about our deal with Saylor. He doesn't trust us, of course. But he needs us; he can't do anything without us. And we need him."

"Then you've got your dad and Evans and Tarryall. What do you need with another gun?"

"To keep Evans in line, for one thing. Evans can't be trusted, and Tarryall will sell out for a dime. You're different. You hate York and you want your own outfit. The only way you'll get it is to string along with us. Besides, if you want me, you'll see this thing through." She smiled softly. "You'll do it, Dan."

"What do we do?" Blake asked gruffly.

"We're meeting tonight at Sutton's soddy. That's about two miles north of the Flying Y buildings. You know where it is."

Blake nodded. "I asked you what we're going to do."

"Be there at nine. You'll find out." She didn't completely trust him. He doubted if she ever completely trusted anybody.

"Are you going to pull Ainsley off my back?" he asked.

"We'll clear you with the law," she said. "He really hasn't got anything against you except Harms' killing.

And you said that was a fair fight. Anyway, Ainsley likes his job. He'll listen to us."

"Your dad won't like having me throw in with you."

"He likes anything I like," she said coolly.

She moved toward the door, but he caught her before she reached it.

"Just remember how the deal went," he said. "I'm not one to stand for a double-cross."

"I'll remember," she breathed. "You play this through and you'll get everything you have coming."

He let her go and stood in the doorway watching her as she crossed the yard to the shed where she had hidden her horse. A minute later she rode away, turning once to wave to him. He waved back and then, swinging around, hurriedly gathered the few things he had left there. He had to get out before the posse showed up. Hazel would probably keep her promise about clearing him with the law, but he wasn't waiting around to see.

He wondered what she had meant by saying, "You'll get everything you have coming." Probably a slug in the back. He had no illusions about Hazel Thornton.

CHAPTER
SIXTEEN

Kerry was too stunned for a while after Dan Blake admitted his real identity to think straight

The first thing she was really aware of was Adam York waving the bag of money under Ben Evans' nose.

"Give me that note, you nickel-squeezing skinflint!" he yelled. "We'll take care of Blake later. Right now I want my note."

The banker went to the vault and brought out the note, marked it paid, and handed it to Kerry.

"Let's go home, Kerry."

"What about Blake?" Evans shouted.

"What about him?" York said. "Ainsley can run him down. That's his job."

"But he came here to break you," Evans argued.

York waved the note. "This is the way he did it."

"Do you mean you're not angry at Dan Blake?" Kerry asked, finding it hard to say the name which had been the equivalent of a plague in the York household ever since she could remember.

"I'll kill him if I get the chance," York said without hesitation. "I fought with Jim Blake for years before Ed Harms killed him. We'd have met on the street if Ed hadn't done it first. I don't want a Blake near me now or ever."

"But Dan has treated us all right since he came."

"He was just looking for a way to stab me in the back," York said. Then he looked down at the note. "I can't figure why he brought me the money. There must have been a catch in it somewhere."

Kerry said no more. Adam York would never change.

As they left the bank, Sheriff Ainsley galloped out of town with three men, apparently all that were available at the moment. Kerry wondered if they'd catch Dan. And if they did, what would happen?

"Pa, Dan Blake said it was a fair fight between him and Ed," she said as they rode out of town. "The sheriff has no right to arrest him."

"He's got every right," York said. "No Blake is going to ride into my country, kill my best man and get away with it."

Kerry looked sharply at her father. "He helped you pay off Ben Evans," she said. "Have you forgotten that?"

"There was a trick to it somewhere. He just didn't get a chance to pull it off."

"He could have taken that ten thousand dollars and run off with it."

York turned to look at Kerry, a scowl wrinkling his craggy face. "How come you're sticking up for a Blake? I don't want to hear any more about it."

She knew better than to persist.

CHAPTER
SEVENTEEN

Dr. Bruce Gentry had watched the action in the street and, though he had seen none of the turmoil behind the doors of the bank, he had a pretty good idea what had happened.

Somehow somebody had figured out that the deeply tanned Clyde Carson wasn't really Clyde Carson from Ohio at all. And when they discovered what Gentry had guessed long ago, that he was really Dan Blake, a man who wore the gun brand like a professional, things had erupted. Judging from the way Blake had come out of the bank with his gun in his hand, it had probably been that gun that had kept things from really exploding.

Gentry watched almost idly while Ainsley hurriedly gathered a posse to chase after Blake. They wouldn't catch him, Gentry thought. Blake was too smart for Slinger Ainsley. Obviously Blake had outwitted Ainsley before, after Ed Harms had been killed. Thinking back, Gentry remembered how Ainsley had talked to the stranger right there in the street of Winner after he had brought in Clyde Carson's body, and the sheriff had never suspected the stranger of being the man who had killed Harms.

Now Blake was on his own, and he probably had Evans, Thornton and York howling for his blood. He'd probably keep right on going out of the country. Gentry hated to see that. Somehow he had felt he had an ally in Dan Blake. Not that he expected ever to get up enough courage to make a stand. But it had been nice to think somebody else hated Ben Evans, too.

It was well after noon when Gentry saw Hazel ride back into town and disappear from view on the other side of the bank building. He wondered where she had been. He hadn't seen her leave town, but she could have ridden out anywhere but on Main Street and he wouldn't have seen her.

The old pain tore at his insides again. He had been coaxed here by Ben Evans with the promise that he could be close to his daughter. It had been a rude shock to find Hazel associated with a man like George Thornton and involved in the crooked deals that he knew were developing. She was bad, all the way through. He had failed miserably in his efforts to raise her right. He should disown her and walk out. But it was hard for a man to turn his back on his own flesh and blood.

Gentry hadn't had a customer all day and he didn't expect any. But he knew he had a visitor coming the minute Ben Evans stepped out of the bank and came down the boardwalk, his face red.

Evans stormed into the doctor's office and faced Gentry. "You're coming over to Thornton's office with me," he shouted.

"Somebody hurt?" Gentry asked, rising slowly.

"There's going to be if somebody isn't careful."

"Want me along just in case?" Gentry moved slowly toward his bag. Something was wrong, and he wanted to know what it was before he was pulled over to Thornton's office. Gentry knew that Evans had brought him to Winner to use as his ace in the hole when the blue chips were down. He had the feeling that those chips were on the table right now and that the hand Evans had drawn was not a good one.

"Stop asking questions and come on. Hurry it up."

Gentry shrugged and picked up his little satchel. He wasn't much of a doctor any more, but there was a certain satisfaction in gripping the little satchel.

He followed Evans out into the street and along the boardwalk to the bank. Evans led the way around the corner of the bank to Thornton's office.

"What good do you think he'll do you?" Thornton demanded when Gentry followed Evans into the office.

"He'll see that we get a fair vote," Evans said, puffing from hurrying.

"We took a vote," Thornton said. "Hazel and I voted to put the squeeze on York right now. No sense in waiting. You're outvoted."

"I won't be this time," Evans said smugly. He looked at Hazel. "If you want your old man to stay in one piece, you'll see things my way."

"Your way is too slow," Hazel said, her face and voice as hard as granite. Gentry found it difficult to believe this was his daughter.

"It won't take long," Evans said. "York is paid off now, but it won't be three months till he'll have to come crawling for more loans — if we make sure he doesn't have any good cattle to sell or enough feed to get him through the winter. That's the safe way. We'll have his land legally in another year."

"We're getting his land now," Thornton said. He held up a paper. "I've studied law, you know. I've drawn up this bill of sale. York's land is all described legally. Once he signs this, there's nothing he'll be able to do to stop us."

"You're going to have a war getting him to sign that," Evans said.

"You afraid of a little fighting?" Hazel asked contemptuously.

"When you tangle with Adam York, you don't get off with a little fighting," Evans said. "My way is the safe way."

Thornton got up from the desk and moved around to face Evans. "We're not interested in your safe ways. We're getting that land tonight."

"You'd better take your vote again, Thornton," Evans said. "Hazel doesn't want to see her old man pounded to a pulp."

"You wouldn't dare do that," Hazel said, her eyes blazing.

"Wouldn't I?" Evans said triumphantly.

Gentry had no warning. Evans brought his pudgy fist around and slammed it against the side of Gentry's face. Gentry reeled against the side of the office and slumped to the floor.

Hazel ran across to him, giving Evans a tongue lashing that would have wilted a drunken cowboy. Gentry didn't try to get up.

Hazel didn't kneel beside Gentry to see how badly he was hurt, but she did take a stand a foot from him, facing Evans defiantly. Gentry felt a warm glow run over him. Maybe she wasn't all bad. There must be a spark of good in her or she wouldn't try to defend him.

Evans had his right hand hooked in the lapel of his coat close to his shoulder gun. "Well, Thornton, how about another vote?"

"I don't care what you do to the old man," Thornton snapped.

"Oh, but Hazel does," Evans said smoothly. "And she has the deciding vote."

Hazel reached down then and helped Gentry to his feet and over to a chair. Evans came over to stand behind the chair, pushing Hazel away.

"How about it, Thornton?" Evans pressed. "From now on I give the orders. Right?" He looked at Hazel. "Did you ever see a man beaten to death?"

Gentry knew what Evans meant, and he didn't doubt that the man was capable of doing it.

Without warning, Evans slapped Gentry again on the side of the head, making his head ring and almost knocking him off the chair.

Hazel ran toward him again, but Gentry never felt her touch. Just before she reached him, she wheeled toward Evans, gripping his right arm.

"Now, George!" she screamed. "Now!"

Gentry saw Thornton dive for his gun. He plunged to one side a second before Thornton's gun roared. From the spot where he was sprawled on the floor, Gentry looked up at Ben Evans reeling back toward the wall as if slammed there by a heavy hand. Hazel let go and watched him fall.

Thornton moved forward, gun held at the ready. "Quick thinking, Hazel," he said.

"Looks like you hit him in the shoulder," Hazel said, as unconcerned as if she were talking about a rabbit. "Going to finish him?"

Thornton reached down and jerked the little gun from Evans' shoulder holster. "I'm going to let the doc do that. He's wanted to for a good many years. Let him have the fun. We've got some papers to look over."

Gentry was still sitting on the floor when Thornton and Hazel left the office. Evans was beginning to howl with pain as the first shock wore off.

Gentry still didn't move, thinking of what Thornton had said. Let the doc finish him. For years he would have given his right arm for a chance to kill Ben Evans. Now he had his chance. Even from this distance, he could see that the wound Thornton had given Ben wasn't going to kill him. The blood that was showing on Evans' coat was high in the left shoulder.

"Doc," Evans panted, "do something."

"Just what do you want me to do?" Gentry asked, getting up. "Find a gun and finish the job?"

Evans looked at Gentry, wildness in his eyes. "Give me something to stop the pain."

"A bullet would do it," Gentry said. He should have been revelling in this moment when Ben Evans was crawling to him for help. But he wasn't.

"Do something, Doc," Evans begged. "This pain is killing me."

152

Gentry looked at the pudgy man in disgust. "Men fought for a whole day during the war after being wounded worse than that."

He went to the satchel where it had fallen when Evans had knocked him against the wall. He opened it. Nothing seemed to be broken.

He lifted one bottle and looked at it speculatively. Laudanum. The best pain killer a doctor could carry. A teaspoonful of that contained enough opium to make a man senseless to pain. Five or six teaspoonfuls would put a man so soundly to sleep that he'd never wake up.

That would be just as good as a bullet, Gentry thought. And if the sheriff did get nosy, who could prove that it hadn't been the shock of the bullet wound that had killed Evans? Nobody but a coroner. And Gentry was the coroner.

"Hurry, Doc," Evans pleaded. "Do something."

What was he waiting for? Gentry thought. He had waited twelve years for a chance to get at Evans. Now he had that chance.

He looked around for a glass and found one. He could give Evans one teaspoonful right out of the bottle. But Evans wouldn't take five without knowing something was wrong. If it were diluted in a little water, however, he'd probably never suspect.

He got the glass and put a little water in it. Not much. Five teaspoonfuls of laudanum added to the water would make a lot for Evans to drink. Gentry put in one spoonful, then stopped. He looked down at Evans writhing in pain. He hated him. Surely no man could hate another more than he hated Ben Evans. But he couldn't kill him. He was a doctor, sworn to save lives, not destroy them.

"Hey Doc," Evans groaned, "are you going to give me that medicine?"

"Sure," Gentry said, and took the glass with only one teaspoonful of laudanum in it.

After Evans had taken the medicine, Gentry picked up his bag and went outside. He couldn't face himself. And he didn't want to be there when Hazel and Thornton came back.

CHAPTER
EIGHTEEN

Dan Blake was back in the sand hills southeast of the Lazy B buildings when the posse rode into the ranch yard. He watched the men close in from the southwest, carefully surround the place, then charge it. He grinned as the men came sheepishly out of the house, and wondered what Ainsley was thinking now. The sheriff had done a good deal of riding for no purpose the last few days.

Blake watched the posse disappear toward town and knew that the search for him was done for today. The sun was gone now, the afterglow burning the western sky. He nudged his horse down toward the creek, his mind running ahead to his meeting at nine o'clock tonight at the old soddy. He wondered what the next few hours would bring.

Ten years of hating Adam York could not be entirely wiped out by his love for Kerry. And no matter what happened tonight, York would never willingly take him into the family.

Before reaching the creek, he reined up to watch a lone rider gallop into the Lazy B yard. He hesitated only a minute, then kicked his horse into a lope toward the buildings.

Dr. Gentry was just coming back to his horse after trying the house when Blake rode in.

"I thought maybe you'd skipped out of the country," Gentry said.

"I was just watching Ainsley and his posse from a distance," Blake said.

"I met them about a mile from here. I turned out so they wouldn't see me."

"There's nobody sick here," Blake said. "What brings you out?"

"There's somebody sick, all right," Gentry said. "It's me. I need the help of a man. I thought you might be it."

Blake shook his head. "I'm afraid I'm not in shape to help anybody. I'm pretty busy keeping one jump ahead of the law."

"I've got something to tell you, Blake, that may change your mind."

Blake swung out of his saddle. "I'm listening."

"First, Hazel Thornton is my daughter."

The kick of a mule wouldn't have shocked Blake any more.

"Thornton shot Evans this afternoon," Gentry went on. "They were in this together to get York's land."

Blake had heard that before. But if Evans was out of it, the odds were getting better.

"Evans wanted to go slow and get York in debt again and foreclose," Gentry went on. "Thornton is set on crowding York out right now. Thornton is an evil man, Blake. I want to get Hazel away from him."

Blake scratched his head. "I don't see how I can help do that. I've got a date tonight to meet Hazel and Thornton at a soddy just a little way from the Flying Y. I think I'll keep that date. Want to come along?"

"Maybe." Gentry sighed. "Are you going to join them in their raid on York?"

"I didn't know there was going to be a raid," Blake said. "But they evidently think I'll go along with any scheme they have to hurt York."

He shot a glance at Gentry. "What about you when the bullets start flying?"

Gentry dropped his head. "I'm no part of a man. I've been trying to get up nerve enough to kill Ben Evans for twelve years. Today I had a perfect chance and I couldn't do it. All I can do tonight is ride along and patch up those who get tagged."

It still wouldn't be unreasonable odds, Blake thought, unless York let his old hate put him on the opposite side of the fence from Blake. If he did that, it would be simple for Thornton to win it all. Blake would have to wait and play his hand when he saw what cards he held.

"Ready to ride, Gentry?"

The doctor nodded. "Sure. If you get a chance, will you get Hazel out of this?"

"I'll be lucky to get myself out," Blake said.

It was nearly nine o'clock when Blake and Gentry rode up to the old soddy and dismounted. The low building was a vague bulk in the darkness. They were waiting — Thornton, Tarryall, and Hazel. Thornton stepped forward, jerking a thumb at Gentry, his voice heavy with suspicion when he spoke.

"What's he doing here?"

"I ran into him down the river," Blake said. "He seemed willing to come, and I thought having a doc along might be handy."

"You let me do the thinking, Thornton said."

"They tried to tell me you wouldn't show up, Dan," Hazel said.

"I still don't like it," Tarryall said sourly.

"Shut up," Thornton said. "He came, so I figure he's riding with us. He's got as much to gain as any of us."

"Just what is that?" Blake said. "I'd like to hear it again."

"Don't trust us, do you?" Thornton said.

"Should I? After the way you were double-crossing Evans, why should I trust you?"

"All right," Thornton said, glancing around. Blake guessed he was checking his support and seeing only Tarryall. He needed Blake. "You get to help break York, which should be reward enough. But you'll also get the sand hill part of the Lazy B and Flying Y, too. Isn't that enough?"

"Sounds good," Blake said.

"Let's ride," Thornton commanded.

A moon was showing in the east now, but the light was too thin for Dan to see Thornton's face. "Just exactly what are we going to do?" Blake asked.

"We'll touch off a few stacks of hay," Thornton said; "maybe a building or two — just enough to make the

158

old fool see we mean business. He gave the same treatment to the settlers. Maybe he'll take the hint."

"You'd better stay here, Pa," Hazel said.

"I think I'll ride along," Gentry said. "I'll stay out of everybody's way."

"You'd better, old man," Thornton said. "We mean business tonight, and we don't want to be bothered by a doddering old idiot who's afraid of his shadow."

They swung away from the soddy and headed directly for the Flying Y buildings. Tarryall fell in beside Blake.

All was dark when they reined up in the meadow below the Flying Y buildings. Thornton gave instructions:

"Hazel and I will fire the stacks. Jim, you stay with Blake and Gentry. Watch the bunkhouse. If York has brought in his crew, we'll light a shuck. If he hasn't, we'll finish the job tonight."

Blake watched Thornton and Hazel ride toward the big barn and the two stacks not far from it. He was more convinced than ever that Tarryall had been told to watch him.

Blake rode up to one of the sheds halfway between the barn and the house, Tarryall and Gentry behind him. Swiveling around in the saddle, he watched Hazel and Thornton at work down by the stacks. They were only vague figures in the thin moonlight until a tiny finger of flame leaped up one side of a stack. Almost instantly the fire spread over the top of the dry hay, throwing a weird flickering light over the yard.

A wild yell came from the house, and a thinly clad figure dashed out into the yard. He ran halfway to the barn, uttering curses at the top of his voice. Blake swung his gaze to the bunkhouse, but it remained quiet. The crew was still in the sand hills.

Blake stirred uneasily. This wasn't the way he had figured it would go. He had thought York would come out of the house throwing lead. But there he was in his nightshirt without a weapon more potent than a loud mouth. Blake had figured York's appearance would even the odds when he made his stand against Thornton and Tarryall. But he was no better off now than before. In fact, he was in a worse spot, for York had been his only hope of help.

Thornton and Hazel had swung back into their saddles at the first yelp from York, and now they came dashing toward the old man. York realized his mistake and wheeled back toward the house, saving his breath now for running.

"Cut the old fool off!" Thornton yelled. "Don't let him get a gun."

Tarryall started to spur his horse away from the shed, then stopped, his eyes on Blake. "Thornton can cut him off," Tarryall said, and held his horse in check.

York had almost reached the porch when Thornton swung in between him and the steps.

"All right, York," he commanded. "Stop right where you are."

The old man straightened and shook a fist at Thornton. "A fire bug! A dirty sneaking fire bug! You haven't got the nerve of a coyote!"

"Shut up!" Thornton said. "You're finished, old man. If you'd had sense enough to pound dust down a rat hole, you'd have gotten out with something. Now you'll be lucky if you don't get your hide ventilated."

Thornton swung down in front of York. Blake dismounted, too, and Tarryall and Gentry followed suit. If there was any fear in Adam York, he didn't show it. Blake felt a flicker of admiration for the old man.

"You fired my stacks!" York bellowed.

"Get rid of that head of steam," Thornton said contemptuously. "This is the same medicine you handed out to the settlers, but you don't like it when it comes your way."

York had taken two steps toward Thornton. Now he stopped as if sensing that the tide had run out for him. He wiped a hand across his craggy face. Murky light from the burning stacks threw weird shadows across the yard. Blake stood motionless, watching, knowing that things had to break soon and wondering where Kerry was. Apparently Thornton had forgotten her.

"I'm offering you a deal, York," Thornton said.

"I won't make any deal with a crawling snake like you," York bawled. He stood very straight, a comical figure in his nightgown, his skinny legs showing below the garment. "Give me a gun, that's all I ask. Just give me a gun!"

"Listen, you fool," Thornton shouted. "You're licked. Can't you get that through your rabbit-brained head? We'll pay you a fair price for your land. You'll sell now, or else you're a dead man."

"I'm not selling!" York choked.

"You'll sign over this land one way or the other," Thornton said, suppressed rage breaking the smooth tenor of his voice. "If you act stubborn, we'll work on you till you'll be glad to sign."

"Go to blazes!" York shouted.

"Ever have a fingernail pulled out by the roots?" Thornton asked. "Or maybe some matches driven under your nails and then fired? I'm an old hand at this, mister. You'll sign, and that's a promise."

"Get the girl," Tarryall said. "Sear up her face a little, and the old fool will sign mighty quick."

Thornton might have forgotten Kerry but Tarryall hadn't. Blake inched back a step, his hand gripping the butt of his gun. This was it. They could mistreat York, and Blake would wait for the most opportune moment to interfere. But if they laid a finger on Kerry, he wouldn't wait another second, regardless of the odds against him.

"Good idea, Jim," Thornton said. "Hazel, get the girl. I should have thought of her before."

York, cursing like a crazy man, lowered his head and charged Thornton. Thornton, apparently taken by surprise by the suddenness of York's charge, went down under the old man. They rolled over and over, York hammering, kicking, biting and gouging like an animal and definitely getting the better of the fight.

Then a muffled shot echoed across the yard, and York stiffened and rolled off Thornton, revealing a smoking gun in Thornton's hand.

162

Thornton got up and holstered the gun. "What else did you expect me to do? Get the girl. I'll fix things so her signature will do the trick."

Hazel started across to the house and was almost at Blake's elbow when Kerry ran out on the porch, a long robe wrapped around her. Apparently she slept in a room on the far side of the house and hadn't been awakened until the shot was fired.

"Hold it, Kerry!" Blake shouted.

He had to make his stand now. The only way they'd ever lay a hand on Kerry was over his dead body. His eyes shot around the yard. Thornton was thirty feet distant, standing not far from the spot where York lay. Hazel was almost at his elbow, and off to his right, in the shadow of the house, was Gentry. The odds were against his getting both Thornton and Tarryall before he was hit. But he had to stay on his feet long enough to get them both.

Everyone in the yard was dead still. Kerry was poised on the edge of the porch like a frightened bird.

Then suddenly there was a violent commotion where Gentry was standing. An instant later, Thornton cursed and wheeled toward the house. Gentry had thrown something and hit Thornton, Blake realized. In that instant, the ranch yard exploded into action.

With his left arm, Blake gave Hazel a shove, knocking her down. His right hand whipped up his gun. Tarryall had come unglued the moment Thornton had moved.

With Thornton's attention momentarily turned on the house, Blake snapped his first shot at Tarryall. He

163

was so close he couldn't miss, the bullet slapping the puncher in the chest and driving him back several feet before he fell. Tarryall's gun didn't fire until he was staggering backward, the slug digging into the dirt inches from his own feet.

Blake felt the burn of a slug along his ribs as Thornton wheeled on him and fired hastily, after realizing his mistake in being drawn away from his prime purpose. Blake took long enough to make sure of his shot, giving Thornton time to fire another shot. But again Thornton fired without taking proper aim, and this time the bullet missed its mark entirely.

Blake quickly fired twice, then waited as Thornton toppled forward into the dust of the yard. Blake wheeled to face Hazel, but she had made no move to enter the fight.

It was quiet then, with the quiet of death, as the echoes of gunfire rolled away into the night and died. Kerry ran across the yard to her father and kneeled beside him, sobbing. Blake crossed to her and stood looking down, not knowing what to say. Adam York was dead.

He heard movement and talking behind him and knew that Gentry was talking to Hazel. But that didn't seem to matter now. All that mattered was Kerry, and grief had pulled her off into a heartbroken world of its own.

Gentry move quickly from one of the fallen men to another. When he rose from York, he took Blake's arm.

"Better let her alone for a while," he said.

Blake followed Gentry back to the porch. "You told me you weren't a brave man," he said. "You know you risked getting killed when you threw whatever you did to attract Thornton's attention."

"I threw a bottle of laudanum," Gentry said. "You wouldn't have had a chance against those two without some help."

Blake looked at Hazel, who stood leaning against the house, shocked into silence as Kerry was shocked into grief, and tried to fathom what all this was going to mean. The sound of hoofbeats broke into his speculation.

Sheriff Ainsley and two men rode into the flickering light of the fire that had now enveloped both stacks of hay but was not threatening any of the buildings.

"I'm looking for Thornton," Ainsley said without ceremony.

Blake pointed. "There he is. What do you want him for?"

Ainsley rubbed his chin. "Nothing now, I guess. I did want him for the murder of Ben Evans."

"Evans dead?" Gentry asked, stepping into the yard.

"A man doesn't usually live with a bullet hole between his eyes." Ainsley said.

Blake wheeled to look at Hazel. With a heavy sigh, she moved forward.

"George killed him, all right," she said. "I suppose you figured it was George who did it because you found his body in our office."

Hazel had dropped all pretense now. Blake noticed in particular that she no longer called George Thornton Dad.

"Evans was all right when I left him," Gentry said.

"George went through Evans' papers," Hazel explained more to Gentry than to the sheriff. "Evans didn't own all that property that Mother got from you at the time of her divorce. Evidently all he got was the cash. Mother must have seen through him and kept everything in her name. Ben had a copy of her will which gives it all back to you, Pa. The original copy of that will is in her own strongbox back in Chicago where Ben couldn't get it. When George found out Evans didn't have all the property he'd thought we'd get from him, he went back and killed him."

"What about this mess?" Ainsley asked, sweeping his hand over the yard.

Blake told him. "You've been hounding me for killing Ed Harms," he finished. "That was a fair fight, just like the one tonight. What are you going to do about it?"

Ainsley cuffed back his Stetson, his eyes sweeping the yard again. "I'll take your word for it, Blake," he said. "But I'll have to take in Hazel Thornton. Seems to me she was tied in with a lot of crooked deals."

Hazel looked across at Gentry. "Are you going to let him take me in, Pa?" she asked.

Gentry looked at Hazel, sadly. "You made your bed, Hazel. Don't blame me if it's lumpy." He looked at the sheriff. "Mind if I ride in with you?"

"Of course not," the sheriff said. "We'll move the bodies into town. And you'd better come into town for a day or two, Kerry."

"I will," Kerry promised.

"Now let's get that fire under control, men," Ainsley said, "then get back to town."

Two hours later, after the stacks had been reduced to smoldering, water-soaked ashes, the posse left with Hazel and Gentry.

Blake turned to Kerry. "I'll get the team hitched to the buggy."

She touched his arm, and he stopped. "Dan, we must get one thing straight. Your father and my father hated each other. I don't know the right or wrong of it and I doubt if you do, either. But I believed Pa when he said he didn't hire Ed Harms to kill your father. Did you?"

He hesitated a moment. She might be right. Anyway, Adam York was dead, and his greedy way of life had brought him no real happiness. It struck Blake then that he had been wrong, that hate and the lust for revenge were even sorrier motives than greed upon which to build a life. Kerry wanted to believe that Adam York had been innocent of Jim Blake's death. Why should he cling to a belief that could do nothing but hurt everyone concerned?

"Sure," he said. "Adam York wouldn't have hired anyone to kill a man. He'd have done it himself if he'd thought it had to be done."

She continued to look up at him until he began to feel uncomfortable. "I should have known all the time that you weren't my cousin," she said finally. "At least I should have known it after you kissed me."

"I didn't feel much like a cousin," he admitted. "Fact is, I never have." He cleared his throat, knowing that he had to say one more thing and that all his future happiness depended on her response. "I love you, Kerry. I don't have anything to offer, but —"

Her hands crept up to his shoulders. "Dan, Dan," she breathed, "what else is there for a man to offer except his love?"

He kissed her then, and it was as if the past had never been.

About Author

Wayne C. Lee was born to pioneering homesteaders near Lamar, Nebraska. His parents were old when he was born and it was an unwritten law since the days of the frontier that it was expected that the youngest child would care for the parents in old age. Having grown up reading novels by Zane Grey and William MacLeod Raine, Lee wanted to write Western stories himself. His best teachers were his parents. They might not be able to remember what happened last week by the time Lee had reached his majority, but they shared with him their very clear memories of the pioneer days. In fact they talked so much about that period that it sometimes seemed to Lee he had lived through it himself. Lee wrote a short story and let his mother read it. She encouraged him to submit it to a magazine and said she would pay the postage. It was accepted and appeared as *Death Waits at Paradise Pass* in *Lariat Story Magazine*. In the many Western novels that he has written since, violence has never been his primary focus, no matter what title a publisher might give one of his stories, but rather the interrelationships between the characters and within their communities. These are the dominant characteristics in all of Lee's Western fiction and create the ambiance so memorable in such diverse narratives as *The Gun Tamer* (1963), *Petticoat Wagon Train* (1972), and *Arikaree War Cry* (1992). In the truest sense Wayne C. Lee's Western fiction is an outgrowth of his impulse to create imaginary social fabrics on the frontier and his stories are intended primarily to entertain a reader at the same time as to articulate what it was about these pioneering men and women that makes them so unique and intriguing to later generations. His pacing, graceful style, natural sense of humor, and the genuine liking he feels toward the majority of his characters, combined with a commitment to the reality and power of romance between men and women as a decisive factor in making it possible for them to have a better life together than they could ever hope to have apart, are what most distinguish his contributions to the Western story.

ISIS publish a wide range of books in large print, from fiction to biography. Any suggestions for books you would like to see in large print or audio are always welcome. Please send to the Editorial Department at:

ISIS Publishing Limited
7 Centremead
Osney Mead
Oxford OX2 0ES

A full list of titles is available free of charge from:

Ulverscroft Large Print Books Limited

(UK)
The Green
Bradgate Road, Anstey
Leicester LE7 7FU
Tel: (0116) 236 4325

(Australia)
P.O. Box 314
St Leonards
NSW 1590
Tel: (02) 9436 2622

(USA)
P.O. Box 1230
West Seneca
N.Y. 14224-1230
Tel: (716) 674 4270

(Canada)
P.O. Box 80038
Burlington
Ontario L7L 6B1
Tel: (905) 637 8734

(New Zealand)
P.O. Box 456
Feilding
Tel: (06) 323 6828

Details of **ISIS** complete and unabridged audio books are also available from these offices. Alternatively, contact your local library for details of their collection of **ISIS** large print and unabridged audio books.